FELIX DASHWOOD AND THE TRAITOR'S

LUKE TEMPLE

Collect all the 'Felix Dashwood' series:

☐ Felix Dashwood and the Traitor's Treasure

☐ Felix Dashwood and the Mutating Mansion

☑ Felix Dashwood and the Traitor's Revenge

Collect Luke's 'Ghost Island' series:

☐ Ghost Post

☐ Doorway To Danger

☐ The Ghost Lord Returns

About the Author

Luke Temple was born on Halloween, 1988. When Luke was a child, he didn't enjoy reading, he was terrible at spelling and found writing hard work. Yet today he's an author! When not writing, Luke spends most of his time visiting schools and bringing his stories to life with the children he meets.

To find out more about Luke and his books, including fascinating facts, fun videos, downloads and hidden secrets, visit his website:

 www.luketemple.co.uk

FELIX DASHWOOD AND THE TRAITOR'S REVENGE

Dear Erin and Finn,

Luke

LUKE TEMPLE

Sept 2015.

Gull Rock Publications

Dedicated to Medieval Mike:
I will find a story for you one day!

With thanks to Jessica Chiba, Catherine Coe, Gareth Collinson, Mike
and Barbara Temple, Kieran Burling and the Highfield Hall Jury

www.luketemple.co.uk

First published in Great Britain by Gull Rock Publications

The paper used in the printing of this book has been made from wood grown in managed, sustainable forests.

ISBN: 978-0-9572952-4-7

Printed and bound by CPI Group (UK) Ltd, Croydon, CR0 4YY

A catalogue record of this book is available from the British Library

Thistlewick Island

Explore an interactive map of Thistlewick
at: **www.luketemple.co.uk/map.html**

1

The White Smoke

Luna Claw watched Traiton's large, rough hand stroke two bottles made of crystallised glass.

'Time to put my plan into action,' he growled.

'Yes,' Luna agreed.

Traiton pulled the cork stopper of one bottle out. The bottle sighed as its contents were released. White smoke swirled up, hung in the air for a few seconds, then shot out through the round cabin window like a firework.

'You are sure this will work, Wrigglesworth?' Traiton asked.

'Oh yes, sir,' replied the ghost that hovered next to Luna.

Traiton uncorked the other bottle and Luna smiled as the second wave of smoke soared over the sea towards Thistlewick Island.

***

Minutes later, Luna was back in her own cabin, hunched over her crystal ball. She needed to make sure everything went to plan. She thought clearly, *The house of Thomas Tweedale*.

An image, at first faint and blurred, appeared in the crystal ball. As Luna concentrated all her energy on it, the kitchen of a small cottage materialised. In it a tall, thin man dressed in a cardigan looked around cheerfully. Thomas Tweedale.

Luna focused her eyes, imagining her pupils were lasers blazing into his mind. She began to read it.

Thomas was happy to be up early – the bright sunlight shining through his windows had made it impossible to sleep in. Thomas had been living on Thistlewick for a week now and couldn't believe how beautiful the island was. He had already explored most of the coastline on South Thistlewick – its rugged rocks, its hidden coves and crystal blue sea – and was on first name terms with many of the friendly islanders.

Of course, from tomorrow he would have to get used to being called Mr Tweedale again.

He walked over to the fridge and felt a few nerves

mixing with his happiness. This time tomorrow he would be putting on his suit ready for his first day as the head teacher of Stormy Cliff School.

He considered the items on the top shelf of the fridge: bottles of creamy milk and gigantic speckled eggs, fresh from Farmer Potts's farm. The second shelf was taken up almost entirely by a giant cod that the fisherman, Oakley, had given him.

An egg, Luna thought. This would test how easy Thomas Tweedale would be to control. *An egg.*

She watched with glee as he reached for a particularly speckled egg and took it over to the cooker.

Now he was thinking about the last head teacher of Stormy Cliff, Frederick Foxsworth. Foxsworth had turned out to be an escaped criminal, whose real name was Tristan Traiton. From all accounts, he had been a brute, scaring the children half to death. Now Traiton was back in prison and Thomas hoped he would stay there for a very long time.

Ha! thought Luna. *If only you knew what is about to happen.*

Thomas was determined to be a good head teacher. He should be firm, of course, but also kind to the children – they had suffered enough.

Luna yawned. She was getting bored of Thomas Tweedale's thoughts as she waited for the white smoke to reach him.

He cracked the eggshell open and poured its contents

into a frying pan. As the egg sizzled away, he hummed to himself.

Just then, Thomas noticed something bright pass through the window. He frowned, but reasoned it was probably just a trick of the light. He picked up the frying pan and tossed the egg around.

A flash of white filled the whole room.

It shone powerfully through Luna's crystal ball and she shielded her eyes. As it faded, she looked back to see the frying pan clattering to the floor.

Luna Claw spread her mouth into a thin, menacing grin. It had worked!

Thomas Tweedale had disappeared.

A Flash of White

Felix slouched on a bench in the Thistlewick market square, recovering from an early morning helping her mum deliver newspapers.

She watched Mayor Merryweather walk past, his thick moustache curled into a smile, his round body bouncing enthusiastically. He was arm-in-arm with Miss Sugarplume, and they were chattering – no doubt about their wedding, Felix thought, which was due to take place that Saturday. Albert the fisherman hobbled along the other way, chasing a seagull that had stolen a fish from his market stall. Felix couldn't help laughing.

Mrs Spindle's clothes stall stood next to Albert's, and at the front of it was a row of school jumpers. Felix's mum had already bought her one to replace last year's, which was full of rips and tears. The thought of going back to school tomorrow gave her a new and surprising emotion – she was looking forward to it … almost.

She wondered what her new head teacher, Mr Tweedale, would be like. Anyone would be better than Tristan Traiton, the evil man whom she, Caspar and Drift had saved the school from earlier in the year.

Felix felt a tap on her shoulder and turned to see Caspar standing there frowning.

'What's up?'

'Have you heard Mayor Merryweather's news?' he asked.

Felix raised an eyebrow. 'That he's madly in love with Miss Sugarplume? That's kind of obvious.'

'No. I heard him talking to Mrs Spindle. The British police just called him.'

'Oh.'

Caspar sat down next to Felix. He bit his lip.

'What is it?' she asked.

'Tristan Traiton has escaped from prison again.'

Felix felt the hairs prickle on the back of her neck. Her eyes widened. 'How?'

'Nobody knows. Traiton was being kept in a secure cell with CCTV cameras, but no one saw him escape.'

Caspar turned away, and Felix noticed a slight shake in his clenched fist.

'Are you OK, Caspar?'

'What if Traiton comes back to Thistlewick?' he muttered.

'Hey.' Felix put a hand on Caspar's shoulder. 'He

wouldn't be stupid enough to come back here a second time. Everyone will be looking for him, won't they?'

'I guess… And he is quite easy to spot.'

'Yeah,' said Felix. 'A large, bald man with a giant letter T tattooed on his neck would stand out in a crowd.'

Caspar still looked tense.

'Did you see Mayor Merryweather and Miss Sugarplume together?' Felix asked.

Caspar nodded. 'They seem really happy.'

'Exactly, and they wouldn't look like that if they were worried about Traiton returning to Thistlewick.' As she spoke, Felix noticed something small and white, like an albino fly, whizzing round her. She batted it away.

A flash of light filled the air, blinding Felix for a second.

As it cleared, she shook her head and looked back to Caspar, but the bench beside her was now empty. She frowned and scanned around the market square, but there was no sign of her friend.

Where had Caspar gone?

3

A Prisoner Escapes

ONE WEEK EARLIER

Luna sat at the grubby table, waiting for Traiton.

She had chosen the darkest corner of the most run-down café in Pucklebury. Anywhere else, a cloaked woman meeting an escaped prisoner might look suspicious, but here they would blend right in. Luna glanced around the café – every other occupant, with greasy long hair and eyes sucked into their sockets, would look at home on death row.

A young, spotty waiter ambled over to her. 'Can I get you—'

Before he reached 'anything', Luna flashed her eyes

at him and he walked away, like he had never seen her there.

The café door creaked open. No one looked up as the shadowy figure loomed above them and squeezed past the tables.

He took the chair opposite Luna.

'You took your time,' she muttered.

'Had to get a change of clothes,' said Tristan Traiton. 'The prison get-up was a bit of a giveaway.'

'So…' Luna prompted.

Traiton rubbed his bald head. 'So the guard just let me out. He unlocked my cell door and held it open for me. The idiot even asked if he should fetch my coat. How did you do it, Luna?'

'He was easy to control,' she said, simply.

'But will he remember?'

'No, I wiped his mind.'

Traiton's devil-horned eyebrows furrowed together. 'What about the CCTV footage?'

'Wiped too. When the guards realise in the morning, they will think they accidentally recorded over it with a late-night repeat of *Deal Or No Deal*.'

Traiton nodded and said through a slight grin, 'I'm impressed.'

'Enough small talk. I've put a lot of effort into breaking you out of prison, so this better be good. My brother told you about me?'

'He was my cellmate. We got talking about how we

ended up in prison. He doesn't remember committing the burglary he was convicted of. Seems to think you hypnotised him into doing it.'

'My brother is a weak excuse for a man,' Luna said coldly.

'He told me you were angry at him, because he said that you are not as good as the Spectacular Seraphina. I got the impression that this Seraphina is someone you would like revenge on?'

'That may be true.'

'But you do not know where she is now?'

'Correct.'

'Well, I can help you with that…'

'How?'

'But only if you help me first.'

Luna leant forwards and repeated more forcefully, 'How?'

'I know where the Spectacular Seraphina lives.'

'Tell me!' Luna exclaimed before she could stop herself. Her heartbeat quickened.

Traiton smiled and sat back in his chair. 'Here's the deal. Your *special* skills will be very useful for a spot of revenge I am planning myself. The place I wish to take my revenge is the very place where your enemy lives. If you promise to help me first, I will take you there.'

Luna's hands started to shake. She clenched them together. It wasn't wise to show just how much she wanted – needed – this.

'Do we have a deal?' asked Traiton.

'Yes,' Luna replied, breathless, 'we do.'

'Can I get you anything?' came the waiter's high voice.

Traiton stood up, towering over the waiter, and boomed, 'I've gone without decent food for too long. I'll have the full English breakfast.'

The waiter gulped. 'But … but it's ten o'clock at night. We stop serving full En—'

Traiton's left hand grabbed hold of the waiter's neck. As if he were a rag toy, Traiton lifted him high off the ground and pressed him against the wall.

'A full English breakfast. Now! Or you won't see another breakfast time again.'

Traiton dropped the waiter, who scurried off, gasping and nodding.

'With extra mushrooms!' Traiton called after him, then turned back to Luna. 'Now, let me tell you my plan.'

4

Fire

Felix wondered where Caspar had gone. He could have slipped off home, worried about Tristan Traiton, but surely he had disappeared too quickly for that. There had been a flash of light – like lightning, except the sky was blue and cloudless – and he had gone.

She rushed down Watersplash Lane, heading for Caspar's home and hoping he was there.

As she ran, the sun slowly set ahead of her, giving Thistlewick a warm, golden glow. She climbed over a stile and went past Crockett Lane, when something made her look back.

It was the cottage on the corner. It had a red glow in the kitchen window. At first Felix thought it was the reflection of the sun. Then she realised the glow was coming from inside – something was on fire!

'Oh great!'

Felix spun around and sprinted back up Watersplash Lane and over to Farmer Potts's stall on the other side of the market. He was also the Thistlewick Fire Officer. She bumped into the customer he was serving and sent the milk bottle flying out of his hand.

'Steady on!' the customer cried as the bottle smashed on the ground.

Farmer Potts looked from the milk oozing across the ground to Felix. 'What is it, girl?'

'There's a fire on Crockett Lane!'

***

Felix stood outside the front door of the cottage holding up a hose, straining her eyes to see through the smoke. She made out Farmer Potts in the kitchen, a sleeve over his mouth as he aimed the hose's nozzle at the fire. After a minute or so, he turned and waved at Felix.

Understanding his signal, she cut through the small crowd that had gathered and went to the side wall of the cottage where the hose was attached to a tap. She turned it closed.

Farmer Potts walked through the front door. He was holding a blackened frying pan. 'I think that's put an end to it.'

'Well done, Farmer Potts!' cried Mrs Spindle. 'You've saved the day!'

'It was Felix who spotted the fire. If she hadn't

fetched me when she did it would have been much worse. Cottages like this are highly flammable.'

'Then well done, Felix!' said Mrs Spindle.

'Bravo!' called someone else, and the small crowd clapped.

Felix looked at the ruined frying pan. 'Whose cottage is it?'

'It belongs to Thomas Tweedale,' Farmer Potts replied. 'Though he wasn't inside, thankfully.'

'Mr Tweedale? My new head teacher?'

Farmer Potts nodded and held up the frying pan. 'It looks like he was frying an egg.'

'Why on earth would he start frying an egg and then wander off?' Mrs Spindle asked.

Felix didn't wait for the answer. Her thoughts had turned back to Caspar and she quickly began walking towards his house, waving goodbye to Farmer Potts over her shoulder.

A few minutes later she knocked on the front door. It was opened by a lady with a large bun of hair and a gentle smile.

'Hello, Mrs Littlepage. Is Caspar OK?'

Caspar's mum frowned. 'I'm not sure, Felix. He's been out all day.'

'Didn't he came back home earlier?'

'No, I haven't seen him since lunchtime. Is everything alright?'

'Yes, Mrs Littlepage. Sorry, it's just me being silly.

Caspar's probably with Drift,' said Felix, not wanting Caspar's mum to panic.

But a twisting feeling formed in the pit of her stomach. Where was Caspar really? And where was Mr Tweedale?

5

'You're very good at picking old, run-down places to meet in,' said Traiton, eying up the dark room they were in.

Luna raised a sharp eyebrow. 'This is my house.'

'Ah… So, that is what you use to control people?' He pointed at the crystal ball on the table in front of Luna; a smoky substance swirled inside it.

'Indeed.' She rubbed it and gentle blue sparks rose up through the ball to greet her hand. 'You said you need a way of capturing people?'

'Yes. Is that something you can help with?'

'I can control them rather than capture, but I know a man who can do that for us.'

'I would like to meet him.'

Luna ran a hand over her crystal ball. 'He is here.'

Traiton looked around and frowned. 'Where?'

The crystal ball glowed a pale blue colour, illuminating the dingy room. Luna pressed both hands on it and sparks shot out of the ball, joining together and growing. They soon formed the glowing white silhouette of a human figure. The glow faded, revealing a thin man surrounded by a shimmering blue light.

Traiton opened his mouth to speak but Luna held up a finger.

More sparks fired out of the crystal ball, growing and mutating into a different shape. As the glow faded, it became a huge, shaggy-coated dog, with slobbering muzzle and bloodthirsty eyes. Like the man, it had a blue shimmer around it.

'Ghosts?' asked Traiton.

Luna nodded.

The dog growled at Traiton, baring its razor teeth. The ghost-man patted its head.

'This dog has the right attitude,' Traiton commented, 'but who's the other one? He looks like a stick insect.'

'I do have a name, you know,' said the man in a nasally voice.

'What?'

'Wrigglesworth, sir, at your service. And this is my dog, Storm.'

The dog was still growling, a low, rumbling sound.

Traiton turned to Luna. 'Can they be trusted?'

'Oh yes. Wrigglesworth may look like a pathetic excuse for a man, but he has done me good service. When he was alive, he created my crystal ball, and its sister.'

Traiton turned to Wrigglesworth. 'Can you shut your dog up?'

Wrigglesworth stroked its thick mane of hair. 'Sorry, sir, he can sense you're a powerful man. Easy, Stormy, easy.' He looked back at Traiton. 'I have something that I think will help you, something that captures people from any distance – a type of smoke I have developed.'

'And what's your price for this smoke?'

'Oh, I am a ghost, sir, I do not need paying. I don't even need feeding. But only I can control the smoke, so I must come with you. I only ask that while I am there you allow me to try out another of my inventions.'

'What invention?' Traiton asked, narrowing his eyes suspiciously.

'The invention that caused my death. I never had a chance to test it out when I was alive. I can assure you that when you see it, you will want to use it.' Wrigglesworth bowed his head and waved an arm in a theatrical flourish.

'Very well, sounds dangerous. We have a deal.' Traiton stood up. 'I have a ship ready and waiting for us.'

'Ship?' Luna frowned. 'Why do we need a ship?'

'I intend to make a grand entrance.'

'Where are we going, sir?' asked Wrigglesworth.

'You will find out in due course. We sail tonight. It will take two days to reach our destination.'

6

The Ship on the Horizon

Felix arrived at the harbour to find Drift sorting through a barrel of fish.

'Dad wants these ready for market tomorrow,' he explained.

'Caspar hasn't been down here, has he?' asked Felix.

'No. Why?'

She told him about the weird flash of light and Caspar vanishing, and the fire at Mr Tweedale's house.

'Isn't it a bit odd that both Caspar and Mr Tweedale have disappeared?'

'I suppose.' Drift shrugged. 'Maybe Tristan Traiton's come back and taken them hostage. Or maybe he's taken them to have their heads shaved like his. They'll both come into school tomorrow completely bald with giant Ts tattooed on their necks.'

'That's not even funny.' Felix stared at Drift. 'So

you've heard Mayor Merryweather's news?'

'Yeah, Dad told me.'

'Traiton wouldn't dare come back here, would he?'

'Nah, he's too scared of me,' said Drift.

'Too scared of your smell, more like.'

'Oi!' He pointed a fish at Felix like a sword. Its googly eyes stared straight at her. She pulled the fish out of Drift's hand and chucked it to a seagull hovering on a nearby barrel.

'Hey! You'll get me in trouble with Dad if you chuck fish to the seagulls!'

But Felix's attention had been caught by something on the horizon. 'Have you seen that ship out there?'

Far out to sea was a huge, old-fashioned-looking ship. It had two tall masts with giant sails coming off them. The setting sun behind it made the ship's dark wood stand out against the golden light.

'It looks like a pirate ship or something,' said Drift.

'Isn't that a bit odd? I mean, most ships these days are made of metal. What's a big wooden ship doing near Thistlewick?'

'Don't know. Tourists?'

'Do you have a telescope?'

Drift sniggered. 'Why, are you turning into a boat spotter?'

She glared at him.

'Dad probably has one in his hut.' Drift disappeared inside it and came out carrying a long object.

Felix took the telescope and opened it up to its full length. Holding the wide end out in her left hand, she pressed the thin end to her eye. In the fading light, she saw a close-up of waves gently rising and falling. She moved the telescope around until the ship came into view. It was so big that it filled the lens. The deck looked empty. She scanned up along the main mast of the ship. At the top was a flag.

Her heart started to beat faster. 'Oh no.'

'What?' asked Drift.

She handed him the telescope. 'Look at the ship's flag.'

He wiggled the telescope around. 'What about it?'

'Look at what's on it.'

'It's a black flag, with a lightning bolt.'

'And when do you get lightning?'

Drift frowned, clearly not following. 'In storms.'

'And what was the name of the ship that belonged to Tristan Traiton's great-great-great-great-grandfather?'

'*Tormenta*.'

'Which is the Spanish for…'

'Storm…' Drift took the telescope away from his eye and stared at Felix. 'But it can't be… I was only joking.'

'I don't think it's a coincidence that Tristan Traiton escapes from prison and Caspar and Mr Tweedale disappear the day before school starts. Traiton is back, and he's got them!'

7

On the Ship

Thomas Tweedale and Caspar Littlepage stood there motionless. Like a pair of puppets, Luna thought.

The black curtain behind her swept open and Traiton walked into her cabin. 'Well?'

'They're under.'

'That was quick.' Traiton strode over to them.

'I'm good at what I do,' said Luna.

Traiton put his square face up close to Thomas Tweedale's. The man didn't even blink. Traiton moved over to Caspar Littlepage and raised an arm, as if to strike him. The boy didn't even flinch. Quite the opposite of when he first arrived on the ship, a trembling mess.

Traiton lowered his arm and smiled at Luna. 'Perfect.

It is time for part two of my plan. Wrigglesworth!'

Luna watched the ghost float through the curtain.

'I am impressed, Wrigglesworth. Your smoke did what you said it would. How exactly does it work?' asked Traiton.

'It came from within a crystal ball, just like the one Luna uses. Trapped inside the ball, it helps the user to locate a person, but once that smoke is set free, it will actually capture the person for you.'

Traiton grunted. 'This smoke could be very useful. Do you have more?'

Wrigglesworth tapped his pocket. 'In here, sir – but it will only do my bidding. The smoke only responds to the last person to use the crystal ball it came from, and this smoke was in one of my own balls.'

'I see. Right then, these two are ready, Wrigglesworth. You can take them to the cell.'

'Yes, sir, of course.' Wrigglesworth bowed dramatically. 'Come along, you two, time to lock you up.'

Thomas Tweedale and Caspar Littlepage did not react.

'You go, Wrigglesworth. They will follow,' said Luna.

Wrigglesworth nodded and swept out of the cabin. The two prisoners didn't move a centimetre.

Luna looked into her crystal ball and focused on their minds. Under her spell, they were blank and ready for instruction.

Follow the stick insect, she thought.

Instantly, Thomas Tweedale and Caspar Littlepage marched out of Luna's cabin after Wrigglesworth.

The Relampagos

'Come on, Felix,' Drift said through gritted teeth.

Felix heaved her oar into the water. 'I don't see why we couldn't have used your dad's boat. It has an engine. It'd get us there much quicker than this tiny thing.'

'Dad's is noisy. This way we can slip up to the ship without anyone noticing.'

It was the middle of the night and they had only a torch to guide them. They'd decided, rather than worrying anyone, to try to rescue Mr Tweedale and Caspar on their own. Felix had told Caspar's mum that they were having a sleepover at her house. Mrs Littlepage had looked suspicious, but simply asked that Caspar was home in time to prepare for school the next day.

'Why Caspar?' asked Drift, as the boat bounced over a wave.

'What do you mean?'

'It makes sense Traiton capturing our new head teacher. But why would he take Caspar, and not you or me? We got him arrested, just as much as Caspar did.'

'I don't know. Maybe it's like you said: Traiton's taken them hostage, and is going to send a message to Thistlewick demanding we give him his treasure.'

'Well, he wouldn't have much luck, would he? All the treasure's gone now.'

They rowed on. The ship seemed to grow and grow in front of their eyes, a monster of the sea.

By the time the small boat bobbed next to the ship they could barely see the night's sky above them, their vision filled with the dark wood of the ship. Felix felt like an ant staring up at an elephant.

There were a few lights shining out of portholes, but it was mainly in darkness.

Drift shone his torch up the ship and came to a metal plaque. 'Look, it's called *The Relampagos*. Do you reckon that's Spanish, like *Tormenta*?'

'If it's Spanish, then I'm guessing it means lightning – to match the ship's flag. How are we going to climb aboard?'

Drift bent down and pulled a long piece of rope from under his seat. At the end of it was a metal octopus-like thing.

'What's that?' asked Felix.

'A grappling hook. I've seen these being used in movies.'

He stood and threw the hook upwards. It soared towards the ship but only reached three-quarters of the way up it. The sharp metal legs of the hook scraped loudly down the side and it landed in the water with a plop.

'Careful, Drift, we can't let them know we're here.'

'It's OK, I think I've got the hang of it.'

Drift pulled the hook out of the water and took aim again. When he let it go this time, it flew much quicker and Felix watched it disappear over the side of the ship. Drift tugged on the rope. It seemed stuck.

'I'll climb up first. Once I'm on board, you come up.'

Drift clenched the torch between his teeth. With both hands on the rope he started pulling himself up.

Felix flicked her own torch on and shone it around. A metre away from Drift's rope she saw something that made her smile, despite her beating heart. She moved over to it, grabbed hold and started to climb up the ship.

As she drew level with Drift, he turned to look at her, then back at his rope, then back at her. 'How did you...?'

'There are steps carved into the side of the ship.'

'Oh.'

Felix grinned at him, lifted an arm onto the next step and pulled herself up with ease.

Before long, her head popped over the side of the ship. Heart pumping even harder, she turned her torch off and glanced around the deck. It didn't look like there was anyone about. She grabbed hold of the railings and jumped aboard.

'Having fun?' Felix whispered down to Drift. 'A snail would be quicker than you.'

He grimaced and heaved himself slowly up the rope. As he neared the top, Felix grabbed the rope and pulled him the rest of the way. He collapsed onto the deck and lay there, breathing heavily.

'Come on, let's get moving,' said Felix.

Drift stood up and tey walked to the centre of the deck. It was quite bare, with just a few barrels scattered around and a large wheel up on the quarterdeck. The sails were all folded up and tied to the two tall masts.

Where is Traiton? Felix wondered, worried he might appear at any moment.

'I guess Caspar and Mr Tweedale will be locked in a cell,' said Drift. 'In the old days, that's where they used to lock prisoners up.'

'Where would a cell be?'

'On the mess deck, maybe,' Drift suggested. 'Or sometimes they're in the hold right at the bottom of the ship.'

Felix could see two doors. One was under the quarterdeck, a grand-looking door with intricate carvings around it.

'That must lead to the captain's quarters,' Drift whispered.

Felix imagined the large, shadowy figure of Tristan

Traiton standing behind the door, but quickly shook the image out of her head.

The other door was more like a trapdoor, about halfway along the deck.

'That'll take us down to the gun deck,' said Drift. 'I don't think this ship has any guns, though. It's too light on the water.'

They found that the door lifted open with ease. Felix climbed down a few steps and found herself in a thin corridor. She started to walk along it, Drift right behind her.

Then there came a voice that sent a cold shiver through her body.

'Is everything going according to plan?' it boomed.

'Yes, sir. Exactly as you had planned it. The prisoners are secured in the cells,' said a quieter, snivelling voice.

Two shadows appeared at the other end of the corridor.

'Drift, I was right – it's Traiton!' Felix hissed. 'What do we do?'

9

The Circus

Luna stared into her crystal ball at Thomas Tweedale and Caspar Littlepage, slumped in a dirty corner of the ship's cell. Finally, after sixty-one years, it felt like she had been able to put her skills to good use.

She thought back to the circus she had been trapped in for every one of those years. The smoke inside the crystal ball swirled to reveal an image of Luna herself, just a year ago, sitting at another table but hunched over the same crystal ball.

Luna stared at this memory of herself inside that grubby little tent the circus master, Colin McVegas, had forced her to perform in. She looked miserable and depressed.

The sign above her read, 'Mystic Luna Tells Your Future for £1'.

But she wasn't like any other fortune-teller – those charlatans who pretended to read people's futures in crystal balls made of cheap glass. No! She used her crystal ball not to read, but to *create* people's futures…

Luna watched her past self look up as a teenager entered the tent, wearing a baseball cap backwards.

'What are you? Some kind of witch?' he whined.

'I am *not* a witch,' she said through gritted teeth.

'Whatever. You gonna read my future then?' He sat down.

She stared at him for a few seconds. 'Of course. One pound, please.'

He chucked a coin onto the table and folded his arms. 'Go on then.'

Luna watched herself look into the crystal ball and remembered how she had already decided that this youth would meet an unlucky fate. She would make sure of it.

She told him all the usual things – when his birthday was, his grandmother's star sign, the name of his sister's pet goldfish. This was enough to impress the usual punters, but this teenager slumped in his chair and yawned.

Finally, Luna said, 'You have exams soon, do you not?'

At this the teenager perked up. 'Yeah! Will I pass them?'

Luna pretended to look into her crystal ball. She saw nothing inside it – she didn't even try to – but said, 'I'm afraid it is not good news. You will fail them.'

The spots on his forehead joined together in a frown. 'Which one?'

Luna looked up. 'All of them.'

In her cabin on the ship, Luna leant back from the crystal ball and the memory faded. She remembered how the week after that meeting, the teenager had taken his first exam. She'd followed him, and used her crystal ball to enter his mind and convince him that he wasn't right-handed, like he had thought for fifteen years, but left-handed. It had been incredibly amusing watching him write unreadable scribble. When his results came out a month later, he had failed every question.

That was how it worked – she told people what would happen to them, then controlled their lives and made it happen. It was an incredible skill, and there she had been, wasting it for £1 a go in a backwater circus, for sixty-one years.

She should have had a great life, a famous life ... but her chance at fame had been stolen from her long ago.

Now, though, she knew the thief lived on Thistlewick Island. Luna would help Traiton with his plans and then she would take her revenge on the Spectacular Seraphina.

Another image appeared in Luna's crystal ball – not a memory this time, but something from the present. A corridor on the ship. Standing there were a boy and a girl. Luna guessed exactly who they were. Felix Dashwood and Drift Castle.

Luna concentrated on her crystal ball and changed the image to look at Thomas Tweedale and Caspar Littlepage in their cell.

Wake, she told them.

The Rescue

Felix spotted a cubbyhole in the wall containing cleaning equipment. She grabbed Drift's arm and dragged him into it. They pressed themselves against the wall behind mops and buckets.

As the stomping footsteps got closer, Felix didn't dare breathe. Tristan Traiton was a dangerous criminal. He came from a long line of pirates, the scariest of which was his great-great-great-great-grandfather, Captain Traiton. Hundreds of years ago, Captain Traiton had hidden his stolen treasure on Thistlewick. Earlier this year, Tristan Traiton, disguised as a head teacher, had come to the island to try to find it. Felix, Caspar and Drift had managed to stop him. The last time Felix had seen him was when he was being dragged away by two police officers. How would he react if he found her on his ship now?

The men got closer and she could hear their voices clearly.

'What is the next part of your plan, sir?' asked the weak voice.

'You will find out soon, Wrigglesworth,' Traiton replied.

Two voices, but only one pair of footsteps, which clearly belonged to Traiton. Why didn't Wrigglesworth have any? Felix peeked out between the brooms. She held back a gasp as she recognised the square figure, wide bald head and dark eyes of her former head teacher. He was half blocking Wrigglesworth from sight, but Felix could see that this man's looks fitted his voice. He was thin and hunched over, grey and pallid. But there was something odd about him.

As they passed by the cubbyhole, she realised what it was. Wrigglesworth was surrounded by an unnatural glow. She looked down as his feet, and saw that he wasn't walking – he was *floating*. Wrigglesworth was a ghost!

Felix pulled back and listened as Traiton's footsteps creaked up the stairs to the main deck. Her heart stopped when she remembered that Drift hadn't closed the trapdoor – would Traiton notice?

She glanced around the corner and saw his feet disappearing up through the trapdoor, onto the deck.

Felix let out a sigh. 'That other man, Wrigglesworth, is a ghost.'

Drift raised his eyebrows. 'Seriously?'

Felix nodded and stepped out of the cubbyhole. 'We need to find Caspar and Mr Tweedale before Traiton realises we're here.'

'Yeah,' Drift agreed. 'If he sees our boat, we're toast.'

Along the corridor, they came to a rope ladder, which took them down to the mess deck. It was completely empty, not even a table inside. There was a black curtain at the other end.

'The cells could be behind that,' Drift suggested.

They crept over, careful to avoid the floorboards creaking. Drift grabbed the edge of the curtain and pulled it back just enough to peek through with one eye. He squinted, frowned, then moved away.

'What—' Felix began, but Drift put a finger to his lips and pointed at the gap in the curtain.

The first thing that hit her as she looked was a vibrant blue colour. For a few seconds it was hard to distinguish anything else. There was a moon-blue carpet and the walls behind the curtain were lined in a shimmering crystal colour. In the centre was a desk, and on that a lamp, which glowed powerfully – blue, of course – giving the entire curtained-off room a cold haze. It was the person sitting at the table that really made Felix gasp, though. A woman, with thick brown hair braided into many different plaits, faced the other way, hunched over something on the table.

Felix looked for a glow around the woman's body, but there wasn't one. She was alive.

The more Felix stared, the more she felt herself being drawn towards the woman. She felt her hand moving up to the curtain and opening it further, allowing her to step through into the blue room...

There was a sharp hand on her shoulder pulling her backwards.

When they were clear of the room, Drift whispered, 'What were you doing, Felix? That woman could have seen you!'

'I just felt ... I don't know, it was strange. This is getting weird. Who is that woman? Why has Traiton got these people helping him?'

Drift was looking down. 'There's a ladder.'

They climbed downwards briskly, not stopping until they came to the very bottom of the ship – the hold.

It was a dingy, cramped, dark place but Felix didn't dare turn her torch on. They felt their way past crates and barrels. Ahead was a faint glow and a line of glistening metal bars.

'That must be the ship's cell.'

Drift nodded. He flicked on his torch and shone it over the metal bars.

Felix saw two people, slumped in the middle of the small cell. Caspar and Mr Tweedale.

'Thank goodness!' said Felix.

She took a step forwards, but froze as a noise came from her left. A low rumble. Was there someone else in the hold?

'Your torch,' she hissed at Drift, meaning for him to turn it off.

But he got the wrong idea and shone it in the direction of the sound – and straight into the eyes of a vicious beast, its black fur raised, its dagger-like teeth bared.

'Is … is that a dog?' asked Drift.

'It's a ghost dog,' Felix said, seeing the glow around it.

'So we're safe, right? A ghost dog can't harm us.'

Felix looked at its bloodthirsty eyes. 'I think it can definitely harm us.'

She gripped her hands into fists as the dog came towards them, a predator cornering its prey. It growled menacingly as they moved backwards, only becoming more trapped between crates.

A cracking noise made Felix jump. Drift shone his torch down and they saw what he had trodden on. An almost-complete fish skeleton.

The growling stopped, and Felix looked up. The expression on its face had changed – it was now panting and looking eagerly from the fish skeleton to Drift.

'Look, Drift, look at the dog.'

Drift slowly bent down and picked up the skeleton. 'Here, boy, fetch!'

He threw it away from them. The dog bounded after it and pounced, but the skeleton slid away. It wagged its tail thoughtfully and tried pouncing again from a

different angle – again the dog couldn't grab the skeleton.

'That'll keep it busy for a while,' said Felix. She turned back to the metal cell. 'Caspar, Mr Tweedale? Are you OK?'

A groan came from them as they stirred. Caspar's eyes ached open and he blinked.

'F-Felix. D-Drift. Where are we?'

'No time to explain. How do we get you out of the cell?' asked Felix.

Caspar looked to Mr Tweedale.

The teacher pointed. 'There's a key. Hanging up on the wall opposite.'

***

They left the dog playing with the fish skeleton and were soon up on the floor above.

Felix went ahead to check the coast was clear, leaving Drift to help Caspar and Mr Tweedale. They were both slow and seemed to be finding it hard to walk. What Traiton had done to them, Felix didn't know.

She held her breath and glanced around a corner, prepared to come face to face with Traiton, but the corridor was empty. She signalled to Drift and he pulled the other two along.

At the top of the next rope ladder, Felix peered up at the floor above. A silvery light was coming from somewhere. A shadow passed quickly through the light and she ducked down automatically, but then recognised its V-shape: a seagull flying past the ship in the moonlight.

She looked back down at Drift, who was trying to encourage Caspar to climb onto the rope ladder.

'All clear. Come on!'

11

All Going To Plan

Waves lapped in Luna's crystal ball. She readjusted the image, like she was looking through a telescope, until the boat appeared in her vision. Felix Dashwood and Drift Castle were rowing it back to Thistlewick Harbour, with Caspar Littlepage and Thomas Tweedale wrapped in blankets next to them.

Luna zoomed in on Felix's thoughts. The girl was worried about her friend. He seemed very quiet, even for Caspar – she guessed he was very tired.

Felix had a thousand questions about what Tristan Traiton had been up to, but that wasn't important now. They had rescued Caspar and Mr Tweedale from under his nose. Whatever his plan was, that had put a stop to it.

'Imagine the look on Traiton's face when he finds out his prisoners are no longer in the cell,' said Felix.

'Yeah, he'll be furious,' Drift agreed. 'Once he realises, he won't stay near Thistlewick for long.'

Luna smiled at this. *If only you knew.*

She turned around, unsurprised to see Traiton standing behind her.

'Well?'

Luna nodded. 'All going to plan. Now leave me. I have work to do.'

She returned to the crystal ball in time to watch the boat arriving at the harbour.

Drift tied it up to the jetty. Everyone climbed out.

Felix took one last look back at *The Relampagos* on the horizon. Luna watched her grinning to herself – Felix Dashwood really did believe she had fooled Tristan Traiton.

'Come on, Caspar, let's get you home,' said Felix. 'See you tomorrow, Drift. And, Mr Tweedale, I'm looking forward to the first day of school!'

Luna focused on Thomas Tweedale.

Nod, she thought.

The head teacher nodded, and they all went their separate ways.

12

Excluded

Felix stretched her face into a smile as she took her seat next to Caspar in the classroom. She had been down to the harbour earlier and there was no sign of *The Relampagos* out at sea. Traiton had gone.

Everyone around the classroom chattered noisily as they waited for their teacher to arrive. Mr Humdrum was ancient and deaf and they were used to him being late in the morning. Often he would be found dozing in the staffroom.

'So, you feel OK after yesterday?' Felix asked Caspar.

He looked at her blankly and just nodded. Felix frowned.

The noise died down around them. Felix turned to see, not Mr Humdrum, but Mr Tweedale in the doorway. He was wearing a green tartan jacket and matching trousers.

'You will all stand when your head teacher enters the classroom,' he said without emotion.

Felix rose off her chair like everyone else. It was a bit odd, she thought – they hadn't even had to do that when Traiton was head teacher.

Mr Tweedale strode to the front, carrying a wad of paper. 'Good morning, children. My name is Mr Tweedale and I am your new head teacher. Unfortunately, Mr Humdrum has been struck down by a terrible, unforeseen illness, so I will be taking your lessons. It will give me a good chance to get to know you all. You may sit.'

The sound of clattering chairs filled the room. Felix stared up at Mr Tweedale. It wasn't just his voice that was emotionless; his face was fixed into a firm gaze. Both he and Caspar seemed to be acting in the same strange way. It might just be that they were still tired from yesterday – but what if Traiton had done something to them?

'To start, I would like to test your academic abilities. Caspar, please could you hand out the test papers?'

Felix watched Caspar stand and, almost mechanically, take the papers from Mr Tweedale. He walked in between the desks, putting a paper on each. Felix could feel the tension in the classroom. Everyone sat there quietly.

Once Caspar had returned to his seat, Mr Tweedale continued, 'This is a timed test. The time is now…' He felt in his jacket pocket and frowned. 'I am sorry. Has anyone seen my pocket watch?' He looked around and no one replied. 'A large circular watch on a gold chain. No? Nobody?'

'There's a clock on the wall, sir,' said Drift from the back of the room.

'Boy, put your hand up if you have something to say,' Mr Tweedale snapped.

Why is he talking to Drift like that? thought Felix. It was a strange way to treat Drift after he had helped save the head teacher last night.

Mr Tweedale looked at the clock. 'The time is now ten past nine. You have twenty minutes to get as far as you can. You will work on your own in silence and must not share answers with anyone else. Begin.'

He didn't say anything else, but continued to stand in the same spot, not moving a muscle.

Felix watched everyone else slowly get their pens out and open the tests to the first page. She groaned – a test on the first day of school!

The first question was easy enough.

'How far must you travel to walk from the southernmost point of Thistlewick Island to the northernmost point?'

Felix had walked the whole length of the island earlier in the year, when she went to find Captain Traiton's treasure with Caspar and Drift. So she knew the answer: four kilometres.

After that, though, Felix didn't have a clue about the other questions.

'How many buildings are there on Thistlewick?' …
'What building materials are used?'

She had expected the test to be about English or maths. Why was Mr Tweedale so interested in what they knew about building materials?

She glanced over to Caspar, who was busily writing at top speed. As soon as she looked at him, Caspar stopped and put his hand up.

'Yes, Caspar?' said Mr Tweedale.

'Sir, Felix is copying me.'

Felix's mouth fell open. 'No, I—'

'Stand up, girl,' the head teacher ordered.

She did, but gave Caspar a huge scowl. Why would he say something like that?

'Is it true that you copied Caspar?'

'No, it's not true.'

Mr Tweedale fixed his cold eyes on her. 'You are lying.'

Felix felt her face go red. 'No, I'm not!'

'And you dare to answer me back. You can have a detention for that.'

Felix looked to Caspar in desperation. 'Caspar, I didn't copy you. Look at my test – I've probably got the last three answers wrong. I…'

'Girl, what is that in your pocket?' For the first time that morning, Mr Tweedale showed some emotion – his eyes widened.

Felix looked down. There, dangling out of her

49

pocket, was a gold chain. With a horrible feeling, she slowly pulled the chain out. On the end of it was a large golden pocket watch.

'I … I don't know how that got there. I promise I never…'

'First you cheat on your test and now you have stolen my watch. Give it here!'

He stepped forward and snatched it out of her hand.

'You are not the type of child I want in my school. I am excluding you, with immediate effect!'

'What…?'

'You are to leave my school, and not return until I say so. Now go!'

Felix stood there in utter disbelief. Then she felt hot anger rising up inside her. She shoved her hands in her pockets to stop herself hitting something.

Felix turned to Caspar, shook her head, then walked towards the door, feeling every eye in the classroom fixed on her. She raised her eyebrows at Drift and he looked from her to Mr Tweedale, obviously as baffled as she was about what had just happened.

When Felix was out of the room, she didn't look back. She quickly left the school and kicked the playground gate open in anger.

***

'Excluded!' Felix's mum yelled. 'Why? What did you do?'

Standing opposite her in the kitchen, Felix shuffled uncomfortably. 'I didn't do anything, Mum, I promise.'

'You must have done something, Felix.'

'He says I stole his watch.'

'Who's *he*?'

'Mr Tweedale.'

'You stole your new head teacher's watch on the first day of term? Why on earth did you do that?'

'I didn't. Someone must have put it in my pocket…' Her voice trailed off. She knew from Mum's thin, pursed lips that it was no good trying to explain.

'Go to your room right now,' Mum said quietly, which was almost worse than her shouting. 'You are grounded until I have talked to Mr Tweedale.'

13

Test Results

'Has the girl been kicked out?' asked Traiton.

Luna swung around. She was getting tired of him walking into her cabin while she was working. 'Yes. Hold on, Tweedale is checking the test results.'

She looked into her crystal ball at the words and numbers on the test papers in front of the head teacher. Her left hand moved over to a notepad, took hold of a pen and quickly scribbled down what she was seeing.

'Well?' asked Traiton.

'We definitely chose the right boy,' said Luna. 'Caspar Littlepage seems to know a lot about the buildings on Thistlewick. The other boy, Drift Castle, was the worst of the lot. He only got one thing right.'

'What was that?'

Luna rolled her eyes. 'His name... But most of the children knew very little. Not that it matters. If we are to succeed, they will just need to learn to obey my instructions.'

'And you can make them obey?' Traiton half asked, half demanded. 'You can use your crystal ball on more than just two people?'

'With my crystal ball I can only control a few people at a time. But now I have full control of Littlepage and Tweedale, I will be able to control the other children through them.'

'And I have your word that you will continue with my plan until it is finished, before you go about your own endeavours?' asked Traiton, his eyes narrowing.

'Of course,' said Luna. 'You have wanted revenge on Felix Dashwood for only a few months. I have been waiting to get my revenge for sixty years. I can wait a few more days.'

'Sixty years?' Traiton spat. 'You don't even look sixty!'

Luna raised an eyebrow. 'Looks can be deceptive.'

The Class of Clones

The clock on the outside wall of Stormy Cliff said it was 2.45 p.m. – still another fifteen minutes until the end of school. Felix hovered by the school gates.

Mum had forced her to stay in her room all day and it had been driving her mad. There was definitely something suspicious about Caspar and Mr Tweedale. They had changed since they'd been on *The Relampagos* and Felix needed to find out why. So when Mum was busy in the kitchen, Felix had sneaked out and run to Stormy Cliff.

She thought about waiting by the gate for her friends to come out – she'd been excluded, but no one could stop her standing outside the school grounds. But she wanted to see what they were doing in class. Was Mr Humdrum now well enough to teach them, or was Mr Tweedale still in charge?

Felix looked around. There was no one nearby watching her and nobody looking out of the school windows. Quietly, she opened the gate and slipped through into the playground.

She passed the climbing frames and over to the wall of her classroom. She tried not to think about being caught – she couldn't imagine the trouble she'd be in. Felix pressed herself against the wall under a window, then she slowly rose up and peeked through.

Closest to the window inside the classroom was Skye. She was reading a large book and scribbling notes on a piece of paper. Rocco next to her had the same concentrated face as he did exactly the same thing. In fact, everyone Felix could see sitting at desks was reading a book and making notes. It was like they were all clones, being controlled by the same brain.

At the front of the classroom stood Mr Tweedale, so Mr Humdrum was still ill – or, if this had something to do with Traiton, maybe Mr Humdrum had mysteriously disappeared.

Felix ducked down as someone came close to the window. It was Caspar – he paced between the desks, looking at what the others were doing and marking ticks and crosses on a clipboard. He made his way to the front and handed the clipboard to Mr Tweedale.

A ringing sound made Felix jump. The end of school bell. Felix quickly ran out of the playground and hid around the corner.

A stream of children soon filed out through the school gate. Felix called out to Caspar, 'Caspar, over here.'

He stopped and turned to face her.

'Are you OK, Caspar?'

He scowled at her and walked away. Felix sighed – surely he didn't still believe she had stolen Mr Tweedale's watch?

A few steps behind Caspar was Drift.

'Drift! Over here!'

He wandered over. 'What are you doing here? If Mr Tweedale sees you he'll be really angry.'

'I didn't steal his watch, Drift, someone put it in my pocket.'

Drift stared at her, obviously unconvinced, and they stood in an uncomfortable silence.

Felix broke it by asking, 'What have you been doing in class today?'

'We've been looking at old maps of Thistlewick and books about how the houses on the island were built.'

'What, all day?'

Drift nodded. 'It's really good fun.'

'Fun?' Felix frowned. 'Drift, you hate doing that kind of thing.'

'I used to find it boring, yeah. But Mr Tweedale makes it interesting. Anyway, I have to go. I need to get home so I can do my homework.'

With that, he walked off to join the others heading

away from Stormy Cliff. Felix watched him go and her frown deepened. Drift never wanted to do his homework after school and hardly ever handed it in. And how could he possibly have enjoyed something as dull as studying old maps and books? First Caspar and Mr Tweedale were acting strange, and now Drift.

Something odd was definitely going on and it had something to do with Tristan Traiton. But why would he want to know about the houses on Thistlewick?

***

Felix walked down the path to her house, about to go round the back. At this time Mum was usually in the living room at the front, watching TV.

'Felix Dashwood!'

Her heart sank. Mum was standing outside the house, her arms folded tightly.

'Where exactly have you been?' Mum asked, storming up to her.

'Nowhere…'

Mum gave her a disappointed look. 'I spoke to Mr Tweedale on the phone earlier. He seems like an utterly reasonable man. I cannot think what possessed you to steal from him. He says that if you admit to stealing his watch and apologise, he will let you return to school.'

'No way! I'm not doing that.'

Mum sighed. 'I thought you would say that. Well,

I would ground you for the rest of the week, but as I clearly cannot make you stay in the house, I have found you something to do.'

Felix looked at Mum suspiciously. 'What?'

'It was Mr Tweedale's idea. Mrs Didsbury down on Featherbed Lane is getting frail and needs help with various things. He suggested that you could go and help her.'

'Oh, Muuum.' Felix didn't like Mrs Didsbury. She was ancient and grumpy. She had caught Felix trying to borrow her boat earlier in the year, and since then had always stared at her disapprovingly. 'Do I have to?'

'Yes, you do. I hope it teaches you that Mr Tweedale and I will not tolerate your bad behaviour. You will start tomorrow morning.'

The
Old
Woman

Luna watched through her crystal ball as Felix Dashwood rang the bell of number 7, Featherbed Lane. The door opened a crack and a wrinkled, suspicious face poked out.

Luna's eyes widened. It may have been sixty years, but she recognised this woman instantly. The woman Luna would have her revenge on.

Luna smiled at her clever thinking. She had put the thought into Thomas Tweedale's mind that Felix should work for Mrs Didsbury. That way both Luna's enemy and Traiton's would be close, so she could easily keep an eye on them.

'Ah, it is the criminal,' the old woman said to the girl.

The temptation to read her thoughts was too great. Luna focused all her energy and thought, *Show me the mind of Seraphina Didsbury.*

The old woman was frustrated. She used to be fit and healthy, but now she couldn't even take her dogs for a proper walk. Her fingers, which used to perform the most complicated of magic, now struggled to pick up a feather duster. She knew she needed assistance, but why did she have to rely on a girl – a thief, no less – to help her?

A rage built up inside Luna. She could start to take her revenge right now and Seraphina Didsbury would never realise. But Luna closed her eyes briefly and took some calming breaths. She would wait. Traiton had brought her to Thistlewick – he had shown her where her enemy lived – and in return, she had promised to help him first.

And, unlike some people, Luna kept her promises.

With a final glare at Seraphina Didsbury, Luna let the image of number 7, Featherbed Lane fade, and focused her attention back on Stormy Cliff School.

Mrs Didsbury

'I will warn you before you step foot into my house that I have placed my valuables out of sight and if you dare to touch anything without my permission I will tell your head teacher. Understand?'

Felix rolled her eyes and didn't care if the old lady saw her. Two days ago she had been called a hero for helping stop a fire, today she was a criminal.

'Yes, Mrs Didsbury.'

The door opened wider, and Felix walked into a dingy corridor. A powerful smell hit her – a mixture of boiled cabbage and wet dog. Mrs Didsbury hobbled along in front of her, the short walking stick she was using making her limp far more than she would have done without it.

They entered a small living room with faded furniture. Three cream armchairs stood on a grey carpet.

The mantelpiece was thick with dust and scattered with black and white photos. Around the room were various cupboards and shelves made of blackened wood.

Felix saw where at least half of the powerful smell came from. Four mangy-looking dogs the colour of dust were staring up at her from a basket they were squashed into below the mantelpiece.

'Sit,' Mrs Didsbury ordered.

For a second Felix thought the old lady was talking to the dogs, then realised Mrs Didsbury meant her. She chose a small armchair that was so soft it felt like it was sucking her in and trapping her. Mrs Didsbury sat on a chair opposite.

'I knew as soon as you ran away from Stormy Cliff School and you tried to steal my boat that you were trouble. Now you steal your head teacher's watch. Whatever next?'

'I didn't run away,' Felix said flatly. 'I got Tristan Traiton arrested. It would have happened a lot quicker if we'd been able to use your boat.'

But Mrs Didsbury wasn't paying attention. She was watching one of the dogs getting out of its basket. It stretched its legs, yawned, then walked over to Mrs Didsbury and whimpered.

'Is it that time already?' Mrs Didsbury asked.

She pulled herself up and shuffled over to a cupboard at head height on the other side of the room. Mrs Didsbury opened it and Felix could see that there was nothing inside. But the old lady searched around, clearly unable to find what she was looking for, then turned back to the dog. It had been sitting patiently behind her, thumping its tail on an area of floor that had been worn through the carpet to the shiny wood beneath.

'Sorry, dog, no bone for you today.'

The dog wandered lazily back to join the others in the basket, apparently understanding every word.

Mrs Didsbury sat back down. 'Now, where were we?'

'Mum told me to come round. She said I've got to help you.'

'Ah, yes. Well, I suggested that you should be locked in a cupboard and fed only bread and water for a week. That is the sort of punishment I would have received at your age, had I ever dared to be so naughty. But Mr Tweedale has other ideas. He suggested that I give you some jobs—'

Mrs Didsbury broke off as another of the dogs rose from the basket and whined in front of her like the first. She got up and opened the same cupboard as before, the dog sitting as the first had, its tail thumping the patch of shiny wood.

Felix sighed, but as she stared into the empty cupboard again, she noticed something at the back of it. It was hard to make out in the shadows of the cupboard door, but it looked like a colourful painting. Why would Mrs Didsbury keep a painting hidden inside an empty cupboard?

'Sorry, dog, no bone for you today.'

The scruffy ball of fur returned to the basket. Mrs Didsbury shut the cupboard and sat back in her chair. She looked at Felix and bit her lip. 'What was I saying?'

'That you have some jobs for me to do,' Felix said, dreading what evil plan Mrs Didsbury might have concocted to teach her a lesson.

'Ah yes, your punishment. I expect you to work hard. I will have no slacking. Let me see… You will start by taking my dogs for a walk.'

Mrs Didsbury got up *again* as *another* dog whimpered at her, and she searched inside the cupboard once more. Felix tried to get a better look at the painting, but the shadow of the door prevented her. She stared instead at the hole in the carpet. From the area of shiny wood the dogs' tails had worn smooth, Felix guessed this routine happened quite a lot.

She watched the dog lumbering back to its basket. These were the laziest animals she had ever seen. Taking them for a walk would be boring, but easy.

'When do you want me to start?'

'They haven't been for a good walk in days,' said Mrs Didsbury, sitting down. 'You will collect them this afternoon at one o'clock sharp.'

'OK.'

'Well, that will do, girl. You may leave. I expect your mother will have more punishments for you when you return home.'

Felix got up and brushed off the dog hairs that had somehow managed to cover her jeans and T-shirt. She looked over and saw the fourth dog standing expectantly at Mrs Didsbury's feet.

She quickly exited the room as Mrs Didsbury went to the same cupboard for the fourth time.

***

'Drift!' Felix called, seeing her friend hovering around outside her house as she walked back up the path. 'What are you doing out of school?'

He half grinned at her. 'I got excluded.'

'Why? Did Mr Tweedale say you'd stolen his prized pencil or something?'

'No, his rubber, actually. But unlike you, I actually did steal it. Apparently his rubber is as special to him as that pocket watch, the way he reacted.'

'But why did you take it? You must have known what Mr Tweedale would do.'

Drift nodded. 'It was what you said last night. You're right – I hate doing homework, and why would I ever like reading old maps and books? At school it felt like I was enjoying it, but once I got home that feeling started to wear off and I wondered why I had been having so much fun. It was only when I got to school again this morning and found myself getting really interested in an article about wooden beams that I knew something was wrong. So I got myself excluded so I could get away.'

'Caspar is helping Mr Tweedale, isn't he?' asked Felix.

'Yeah, Caspar kept asking about all the information we were finding out. Then he went and whispered it to Mr Tweedale.'

This confirmed what Felix had been thinking. 'Something happened to Caspar and Mr Tweedale when they were on *The Relampagos*.'

'But you said we stopped Traiton from doing whatever he was planning,' said Drift.

'I've been thinking – what if … what if Traiton *wanted* us to rescue Caspar and Mr Tweedale?'

'What do you mean?

'Think about it: we got them off the ship without anyone trying to stop us. Maybe that was Traiton's plan. He could be blackmailing them and getting them to do something on Thistlewick for him.'

'So by rescuing them, we've brought them back so they can carry out Traiton's plan?' asked Drift.

'Exactly. And I bet Traiton got Caspar to put Mr Tweedale's watch in my pocket, so I'd be excluded and wouldn't get in his way.'

'But why would Traiton want everyone at Stormy Cliff to look at old maps and books about buildings? That's all Mr Tweedale has been making us do.'

'That's what I can't figure out. And why is everyone so interested in doing the work?' Felix wondered. 'I watched you all through the classroom window yesterday – you were like robots, turning the pages and making notes.'

'Maybe Traiton is trying to bore us to death.'

Felix half smiled at his joke. 'I wish Caspar was with us – we need his brains.'

'It's no good talking to Caspar,' said Drift. 'If Traiton has done something to him, we can't trust him any more.'

'Can we trust any of the others?'

Drift scratched his head. 'I don't know. But we might be able to speak to them – Mr Tweedale is taking the class on a field trip this afternoon.'

'Where to?'

'Not sure. But we could follow them and find out.'

'Actually, I'm meant to be taking Mrs Didsbury's dogs for a walk this afternoon. We can use the dogs as an excuse for walking around Thistlewick.'

'Why are you walking Mrs Didsbury's dogs?' asked Drift.

'It's part of my punishment. You can tell your parents it's your punishment too.'

'That's a punishment?'

'I know, easiest punishment ever.'

They agreed to meet up after lunch, at the gates of Stormy Cliff.

17

Not Part of the Plan

Luna opened the door of Traiton's cabin.

For a second she thought it was empty, then saw him lazing in his hammock.

'What is it?' he asked.

'Drift Castle has been excluded.'

Traiton sat up. 'Why? That was not part of the plan.'

'He was asking for it. We made it look like the girl stole something, but Drift Castle actually did.'

'What did he steal?'

'A rubber.' Luna chuckled.

'You got him excluded for stealing a rubber?' Traiton climbed out of his hammock and rose to his full height above Luna.

'The boy was useless. He was far slower than the others and kept asking questions. We don't need him,' Luna muttered.

Traiton's eyes narrowed. 'But he will tell the girl what they have been doing in class. About the field trip this afternoon.'

Luna stared up at him. She wasn't scared – she had known men far worse. 'None of the class know why they have been studying the books and none of them know what the field trip is for. Drift Castle is an idiot. He won't be able to figure it out.'

'The girl will want to follow our every move.'

'True,' said Luna.

Traiton ran a finger down the giant T tattooed on the back of his neck. 'Very well. It is no matter if they watch what the class are doing. It will only frustrate them when they can't figure it out. Just make sure that the girl does not interfere.' He stared at Luna and his eyes flashed black. 'And do not go against my orders again. If this is to work, you must follow my plan exactly. Understand?'

Luna nodded coldly.

'Now, fetch Wrigglesworth. I have found a purpose for the invention he is so keen to use – the one he died making.'

'Yes, *sir*,' Luna replied sarcastically, then left him.

Spying

'Where did you get to?' asked Drift, standing outside Stormy Cliff. 'I've been waiting here for ages.'

'It's these dogs,' Felix replied, pulling a twig out of her hair. 'They're the laziest creatures in front of Mrs Didsbury, but as soon as she was out of sight they completely changed. As I walked onto Spinney Lane, two of them turned left, the other two went right. Then they all saw a rabbit and chased after it. They may only be small, but they're strong. All four started pulling me backwards!'

'Like a waterskier pulled by a speedboat?' asked Drift.

'Except this speedboat was a giant ball of fur, and the water was a hard dirt track,' Felix groaned. 'The rabbit shot into a hedge and the dogs all pounced, sending me flying face first through it. It took me ages to untangle their leads and get them to walk in the same direction.'

Drift grinned at her.

'I've changed my mind,' she told him. 'This is a really bad punishment.'

'Hello,' said Drift as the dogs all jumped up at him, tails wagging. 'What are their names?'

'I don't know. Mrs Didsbury just calls them all "Dog".'

As soon as Felix said this, they all turned to look at her expectantly.

'No,' she said firmly. 'No bones. Bad dogs.'

They started whimpering at her loudly.

'They're not going to be like that when we're spying on Mr Tweedale, are they? They'll give us away,' said Drift.

'They'll have to be OK. Mrs Didsbury expects me to keep them out for at least two hours. What's going on in class?'

'They should be coming out any minute.'

Felix heard the familiar scraping of chairs – everyone in the classroom was getting up. She gave Drift the leads of two dogs and they all moved out of sight around the corner. It wasn't as hard to get two dogs to go in the right direction, compared to all four, but it still took quite a bit of tugging.

A minute later, they saw the tall figure of Mr Tweedale walk down the path away from the school, followed by an orderly line of children. Some carried bags and a few held a long ladder.

What do they need that for? Felix wondered.

The children walked in step with each other, not saying a word. Caspar was at the front of them, glancing around cautiously.

What has happened to him?

Once the class were far enough away, Felix and Drift set off down the path with the dogs.

Mr Tweedale took a right turn down a small lane and the class followed. They weaved in and out of different lanes that got thinner as they headed towards the eastern edge of the island, where all the old-fashioned wooden houses were. Felix and Drift kept their distance, which was hard work, because the dogs were pulling on their leads, all the time trying to go faster.

The class stopped at the final house on Seaview Lane.

'Why have they stopped there? No one lives in Tumbledown House any more,' said Felix.

She watched as Mr Tweedale took out a large map and studied it closely. He nodded and gave Caspar an instruction. In turn, Caspar talked to Skye and Rocco, who started to pull something out of a long, thin bag.

'It's an axe!' said Drift.

'What are they going to do with that?'

Caspar pointed to a wooden beam, which held up the right-hand edge of Tumbledown House. Together, Skye and Rocco swung the axe and embedded it into the beam.

'This is mad! Are they chopping the house down?'

After a few hits of the axe they stopped. Caspar stepped forwards and pulled a chunk of the wood out. He threw it into a bag that Braden was holding open.

With that, Mr Tweedale turned around and started to head back along the lane. Felix and Drift quickly dragged the dogs down the side of a house and waited until the class had passed them.

'Looks like they're heading for the market. Shall we keep following?' asked Drift.

Felix nodded.

Drift was right – the class were making their way towards the market square. They found them there, setting up the ladder outside Felix's mum's newsagent's. Rocco climbed up, reached towards the thatched roof and pull out a handful of thatch.

'What are they going to do with that?' Felix wondered.

Soon the class followed Mr Tweedale back to the west of the island. Felix, Drift and the dogs continued to trail them.

'Are they going back to school already?' asked Drift.

But the class walked straight past the school, towards the western edge of the island.

'All the buildings on this side of Thistlewick are made of brick,' Drift explained. 'I read about it yesterday. Are they going to remove a brick from a house next?'

But the class didn't stop at any houses. They kept going until they reached Burnt Tree Beach. Felix and

Drift stayed at the top of the cliff and watched the class climb down it. They all followed Mr Tweedale into a cave below.

'I think that cave stretches really far back into the island. Yesterday, I read that it goes right under Stormy Cliff,' said Drift.

'When they climb up off the beach, let's go into the cave and see if we can find what they were doing,' Felix suggested.

Felix and Drift sat down on the cliff edge and let the dogs sniff around the grass. Felix kept a close eye on the beach below, waiting for the class to come out of the cave. She watched two seagulls start fighting on the sand.

Before she knew it, one of the dogs' leads slipped out of her fingers and the dog shot towards the edge of the cliff – it had seen the seagulls too. It started to stumble down the cliff face, whimpering. Felix stared in alarm – she would be in so much trouble if she let one of Mrs Didsbury's dogs fall to its death.

Fortunately, the dog was more nimble than it looked. It found its footing and managed to edge its way down the cliff, jumping the last few metres. Barking its head off, it charged at the seagulls, which instantly flew away.

Someone appeared at the cave entrance. Caspar. He must have heard the noise. The dog saw him and trotted over. As it got closer to Caspar, it started to growl at him. Even from the top of the cliff, Felix could see its bared teeth. It was going to attack Caspar!

She was still angry with him, but she couldn't let that happen.

'Hold on to the other dogs,' she told Drift. 'I'm going down.'

Felix hurled herself off the top of the cliff and felt her feet slipping on smooth rock. She tripped and tried to grab hold of something, but couldn't stop herself rocketing down the cliff face. The next thing she knew she'd landed on her side on a rock sticking out halfway down. Ignoring the pain, she stood up and saw the beach wasn't that far below. She leapt down and landed on the soft sand.

She took in the terrified look on Caspar's face. However horrible he had been to her, he was still her friend, and he was frightened.

He saw Felix and called out, 'Felix? Help me, please!'

'Dog,' she called, 'stop it!'

The dog ran over to Felix, making a high-pitched whimper, and hid behind her leg. It looked like it wasn't just Caspar who was scared of the dog – the dog was scared of Caspar too. But why?

As soon as the dog had turned away from him, Caspar's face hardened and he stared straight at Felix.

19

Losing Control

Luna breathed a sigh of relief. She had just got Caspar back under her control. But why had she lost him? He had been scared of the dog. That fear must have been greater than her powers and had overtaken them.

She leant close to the crystal ball and focused on Caspar's mind.

'What are you doing here?' she made him say.

'Caspar, no. Why are you being like this?' Felix pleaded.

Another dog suddenly appeared next to her.

Caspar looked up at the cliff and Luna followed his gaze. Drift Castle was standing there.

He called down, 'Sorry, I couldn't stop it!'

'Idiot boy!' Luna spat. She stared deep into Caspar's mind and told him, *The dog must not worry you, Caspar. It will not attack. You are greater than the dog.*

But as it leapt towards Caspar, the scared expression returned to his face. Luna felt herself being pushed out of his mind, the force of his fear travelling through the crystal ball and sending her falling backwards off her chair.

She gathered herself and got back up in time to hear the girl ask, 'Why did you tell Mr Tweedale I was copying you?'

'I'm sorry, Felix. It wasn't … I didn't mean…'

The girl glared at Caspar. 'It was you who put his watch in my pocket, wasn't it?'

Luna had to get back control of Caspar. The girl was starting to figure things out and, without Luna in his mind, Caspar would tell her everything. Luna forced all her energy into the crystal ball.

HEAR ME, CASPAR! her mind yelled. But it was no good.

The girl continued, 'Did you put it into my pocket when I sat down next to you?'

'Yes,' Caspar replied. 'I'm sorry, Felix. I'm really sorry. But, please, get the dog away from me!'

'Dog! Come here!' Felix called to it.

The dog joined the other one behind Felix's leg.

Luna was instantly able to get back inside Caspar's mind. She relaxed as she saw his expression harden.

'Go away, Felix. You're not my friend any more. I hate you.'

The girl frowned. 'That's not you talking, Caspar, I know it isn't.' She looked up to Drift Castle on the cliff. 'Let the other two dogs come down.'

Luna watched Drift hesitate for a moment, then let go of their leads. They scampered down onto the beach and began snarling at Caspar. He pressed himself tightly against a rock at the side of the cave.

Luna quickly removed herself from his mind before she was forced out again. She cursed under her breath. There was no way she could control Caspar with those dogs around. She had to find a way to get rid of Felix and the dogs – and quickly, before Caspar gave the game away.

She abandoned him, and thought, *Into the cave*.

The image in the crystal ball faded and a new one appeared. Now she was inside the cave with Thomas Tweedale and the class.

She focused on the head teacher's mind.

20

Wedding Plans

'Felix, please! Get them away from me!'

The dogs could obviously sense something odd about Caspar. He was acting like two different people – like he was under some sort of spell. Mostly cold and unemotional, but when he became scared he turned back into the Caspar that Felix knew.

'Sorry, Caspar, I need answers. Is Tristan Traiton blackmailing you?'

'No … not exactly. W-what's going on?'

'What happened to you when you were on his ship?'

Caspar gritted his teeth. 'I … I can't say. Please, take the dogs away.'

They were edging closer to him, their snarling getting deeper. Felix had to fight very hard to stop herself calling the dogs off. She knew that the second Caspar stopped being scared, he would change back to being robot-like.

'Where is Traiton? Is he still near Thistlewick?'

Caspar's eyes shut. His whole body shook, as if he was fighting something inside him that was stopping him from speaking.

'His ship … is … just off a cove … close to the forest in the north,' he finally managed.

At that moment another person stormed out of the cave behind him. Mr Tweedale. Felix froze. The dogs fled from Caspar towards Felix at the sight of the head teacher.

'What on earth is going on? You!' The head teacher pointed at Felix. 'You are excluded. You have no right to be here! I have a good mind to…'

Felix didn't hear any more. She took one last look at Caspar, who had changed back to the person she didn't recognise, then ran up the cliff face, the dogs rushing after her.

***

'What do we do now?' asked Drift, once they were well away from Burnt Tree Beach.

'If Traiton's ship is still here, then we need to get back on it. That's the only way we'll find out what he's up to. Could we row there?'

'It's the middle of the day. My dad will go mad if I take a boat out, especially now I've been excluded.'

'But we need to get to that ship.'

'I know Dad keeps an inflatable dinghy in the harbour hut for emergencies. There's no way it would survive being rowed all the way around the island, but we could walk to the north, find where the ship is and use the dinghy to row out to it.'

'Good plan. But first, I need to return these dogs to Mrs Didsbury.'

'I'll go and get the dinghy and meet you back here.'

***

'Hello, thief,' was the greeting Felix got when Mrs Didsbury opened the door. 'Bring the dogs into the living room. I expect best behaviour from you – I have special visitors.'

Once again, Felix wasn't sure whether the old lady was talking to her or the dogs. As the dogs followed Mrs Didsbury through the house, they instantly changed from overexcited rats to the slug-like creatures they had been the first time Felix had met them.

In the living room sat Mayor Merryweather and Miss Sugarplume. One by one, the dogs let out a big yawn, then climbed back into their basket.

'Hello, Felix,' the mayor said enthusiastically.

He was wearing a bright purple waistcoat and his giant moustache sparkled so much Felix was sure he had glitter in it. He really did stand out compared to the room around him, which was drab and colourless.

Felix smiled. It still seemed bizarre that the mayor was getting married. He was really old, and Miss Sugarplume didn't seem that much younger.

'Did you have a good walk with the dogs?' asked Miss Sugarplume. She was, as usual, dressed in a frilly, flowery dress.

'It was … eventful,' replied Felix.

'Does the thief want some tea?' asked Mrs Didsbury.

'Mrs Didsbury, we do not need to be quite so harsh to Felix. I am sure she is sorry for what she did,' said the mayor. 'And she was a great help the other day with Thomas Tweedale's fire.'

'Fine. Well, do you want tea, girl?'

'No, it's OK. I have to go…'

'You children are in such a hurry these days,' said Miss Sugarplume. 'I am sure you can spare us five minutes. We have been talking about our wedding.'

Felix looked at the clock anxiously – the sooner she and Drift got to *The Relampagos* the better. But Mrs Didsbury pulled up a hard chair and pushed her down onto it. A cup of muddy-looking tea was thrust into her hands.

'So … er … are you ready for getting married?' she asked uncomfortably.

'Oh, certainly! I am so excited about becoming this handsome man's wife tomorrow.' Miss Sugarplume beamed and the mayor blushed.

Felix couldn't stop herself from cringing.

'Mr Tweedale has very kindly offered to provide us with a choir to sing at the wedding,' said Mayor Merryweather. 'Most of the children from Stormy Cliff will be involved. You won't be allowed to join in, I suppose? Such a pity, such a pity.'

Felix felt quite relieved that she wouldn't have to be part of the choir – she hated singing. She changed the subject. 'Have you heard anything else about Tristan Traiton escaping?'

'Isn't that awful news?' said Miss Sugarplume. 'There were no broken bars, no tunnel, just no way he could have escaped. How on earth did he do it?'

Mayor Merryweather shook his head gravely. 'I haven't heard anything else. No one seems to be able to find him. But I have asked the police to keep me informed about their investigation into his whereabouts. Like they say, though, he won't be foolish enough to come back here. We are safe.'

Felix almost said something, but stopped herself. If Traiton was sitting just off the coast of Thistlewick planning something evil, she needed to find out what it was before she told people. She looked at the clock again.

'They'll find the man and lock him up for life before long,' said Mrs Didsbury. She turned to Felix. 'It is a slippery slope, young girl. A little bit of thievery now might seem harmless, but look where it can lead you.'

21

Problem

Traiton studied the completed map stretched over his desk. 'The field trip was a success, then.'

'Yes,' said Luna. 'Thomas Tweedale will bring over everything the class collected for Wrigglesworth to examine. But we have a problem.'

Traiton raised an eyebrow. 'What?'

'They know...'

'Know what? Speak plainly.'

'The girl and the boy know we're still here. I think they will try to find us.'

Traiton slammed a fist against the desk, sending a bottle of red ink crashing to the floor. 'How?'

'Caspar Littlepage ... I lost control of him.'

Traiton rose to tower above her.

'Only briefly!' she added.

'I thought you were good at your job. I thought you could handle this easily. Your crystal ball is powerful, you said.'

With each sentence, Traiton pushed Luna backwards, until she was cornered. Her eyes became slits and, for a second, she thought about entering his mind – forcing him to show her the respect she deserved.

'You are the one who insisted on sailing round to North Thistlewick. I told you that the further away I am, the less control I can hold over them.'

Traiton snarled at her, but took a step back.

'We couldn't have hung around in the south in plain sight, could we?' he muttered. 'This cove was our best option, so we could stay close enough, but well hidden.'

He moved back to the desk.

'What has happened, has happened,' said Luna. 'The girl knows, we cannot change that.'

'No. If she is coming, then it is earlier than we had planned for, but we can make it work.' He nodded. 'We will be ready for their arrival. I will ask Wrigglesworth to prepare another bottle.'

Inside Traiton's Cabin

The sun dipped down towards the horizon, its rays spreading over the farmers' fields and nearly blinding Felix and Drift as they walked out of the forest and into North Thistlewick.

Drift held up a small map and pointed. 'We need to go there.'

'You're sure it'll be in that cove?' asked Felix.

'I spent two days studying maps of Thistlewick. I think I know the island blindfolded now,' said Drift. 'That's the best place to hide a ship.'

He guided them along the border of the forest. The trees became more spread out until they disappeared altogether. Felix and Drift moved up to the edge of a cliff.

Felix looked down and grinned at the sight of the large, wooden ship. The sun had set behind it, turning it into a giant silhouette. 'You were right.'

'I don't think we'll need my inflatable boat, it's so close to the beach!' said Drift.

Drift stepped towards the edge of the cliff and was about to climb down.

'Hang on.' Felix held him back. 'Someone's just walked onto the deck.' She stared at the shadowy figure. 'It's not Traiton. Who is it?'

'Mr Tweedale, I think.'

Drift was right. Felix recognised his tall outline as he climbed down from the ship and walked along the cove.

'What is he doing back on *The Relampagos*?'

'I think he's coming our way,' said Drift. 'We should probably hide.'

Felix nodded. They squatted behind a nearby bush, keeping as still as possible. Sure enough, a minute later, Felix saw Mr Tweedale's head poking over the edge of the cliff. He clambered up and walked straight past them, an unreadable expression on his face.

'What is Traiton using him for?' asked Drift, when the head teacher was well out of earshot.

'Let's go and find out.'

Felix and Drift slid out from behind the bush and climbed down the cliff face as quietly as possible. There were hardly any foot- or handholds to grip onto, but Drift and Felix were used to climbing the rocks around Thistlewick, and soon Felix jumped down onto the soft sand. Drift leapt off close behind, and a few strides later they reached the ship.

Half expecting to see Traiton staring down at her from above, Felix's heart raced as she located the steps carved into the side.

There was no one around when she got to the deck. Drift appeared next to her.

'Didn't you say that door must lead to the captain's cabin?' Felix pointed to the door with intricate carvings around it, under the quarterdeck.

'Yep. Do you reckon that's what Traiton uses as an office?'

'Must be,' said Felix.

She crept over to the door and peered through the glass. The cabin was in darkness and the glass was the cloudy sort you couldn't see through properly. There was no way of telling if Traiton was in there.

Felix took a deep breath and grabbed hold of the door handle. The door creaked open and she tentatively stepped in.

'Hello?' she asked, in as normal a voice as she could manage.

No reply.

She flicked on her torch and shone it around. Moonlight flickered through tall stained-glass windows at the back of the cabin, onto a hammock tucked away to the left. Felix shone her torch into it. There was no one sleeping there.

Surrounding the hammock were various deadly-looking weapons – pistols and guns, long, sharp swords, chains, balls with spikes on, and more. A large wooden desk stood in the centre, and behind this were several shelves filled with books and bottles.

Felix beckoned to Drift. 'There's bound to be something here that will give away what he's up to,' she whispered.

Laid out on top of the desk was a large map of Thistlewick Island. It had been drawn in great detail using the blackest of inks.

'Eugh, looking at that makes me sick,' said Drift. 'I don't want to see another map of Thistlewick ever again.'

He went over to the shelves behind the desk and started picking things up.

All across the map, Felix saw that there were red crosses – at least a dozen of them, some in North Thistlewick, but most in the south.

'Look, Drift.'

He glanced over. 'Kind of like a treasure map.'

Felix looked at the crosses more closely. One was drawn over Seaview Lane, one over the newsagent's. These were the places the class had visited earlier that day. There was even a big cross over the cave on Burnt Tree Beach.

'You might be right.'

Drift came and stood beside her. 'But why would the class have been chopping bits out of the buildings if Traiton's trying to find more treasure?'

'Yeah, that doesn't make sense.'

Felix looked at Drift and saw he was holding a round glass bottle.

'What's that?' she asked.

'Just a bottle. There's nothing inside. But look, it's got "Thomas Tweedale" written on it.'

'Where did you find it?'

'On the shelf over there.'

Felix went over to where he pointed. There were two more bottles. She pulled one towards her and turned it around in her hand. Written in spidery letters carved into the bottle, was another name: *Caspar Littlepage*.

'So Traiton did do something to Caspar and Mr Tweedale when they were on the ship.' Felix frowned at the bottle. 'What do you reckon was in this? Poison?'

'Don't know.'

Felix slowly put Caspar's bottle back down, her head reeling at the thought of Caspar being poisoned. There was still one more bottle sitting on the shelf. Who was that one for? Unlike the other two, this third one had a cork stopper in it, and there was something swirling around inside.

She picked the bottle up and turned it around. She gasped when she read the name carved into it: *Felix Dashwood*.

'This bottle's meant for me!'

She went to put it down, but couldn't. Her hand started to shake. But no, it wasn't her hand that was shaking – it was the bottle. Whatever was inside it started to glow.

'What's happening?' asked Drift.

'I … I don't know!'

The bottle vibrated more violently and got hotter and hotter. Felix's hand started to burn, but she couldn't let go. The glow from the bottle grew until it was a blinding white light. Felix shielded her eyes. It got hotter still.

'Arrrgh!'

She managed to rip her hand away and the bottle fell to the floor and smashed.

Before Felix could take a breath, white smoke rose up through the shards of glass. It stretched out towards her like many ghostly hands. Terrified, she backed away, but the smoke followed.

She made a run for it, around the other side of the desk and towards the cabin door. But it was no good. The white-smoke hands shot towards her, curling around her like rope and pulling her backwards.

Drift ran to help, but one of the smoky hands stretched out and slapped him away, sending him crashing into the cabin wall.

Felix kicked and fought against the smoke but it was too strong. It dragged her over to a chair and forced her to sit down. Her hands were pressed firmly to her sides and the smoke somehow tied her to the chair. She looked up at Drift. He was leaning against the wall, open-mouthed.

'Run, Drift, run!'

'But…' He came towards her and tried to pull away the smoke. 'Aaahhh!'

His hand shot backwards like it had been electrocuted.

'Don't try to help me, Drift. Just get off this ship!'

'I can't leave you like this! What if Traiton finds you?'

'You need to get help. Go, before you get trapped too!'

Drift looked anxiously at Felix, then nodded. He threw open the cabin door and ran out.

Felix sat there, breathing deeply, trying not to panic. She felt her chest tightening as the smoke squeezed her, like a snake teasing its prey. She kicked and squirmed, but there was no way she could get out of this.

A thudding sound came from outside. Footsteps.

The door creaked open.

'Get off me! Let me go!' a voice cried.

It was Drift, being dragged back into the cabin. A thick arm gripped him firmly around the neck.

Felix looked up in horror at the tall man who had hold of Drift.

At the bald head.

At the menacing, black eyes.

Tristan Traiton.

23

Free

Luna stepped into the cabin behind Traiton. She smiled as she saw Drift Castle struggling in his grip and Felix Dashwood fighting against Wrigglesworth's white smoke.

'Do you want me to get them under control?' she asked Traiton.

'No,' he replied firmly. 'I want her fully awake for this.'

He kept a straight face, but Luna could sense his intense glee. She knew that it was Felix Dashwood whom he blamed for stopping him getting his treasure. It was the girl he most wanted to get revenge on.

She stopped squirming and her eyes met Traiton's.

'What is the treasure map for? Why are you here, Traitor Traiton? All your treasure is gone, you know. We gave it back to the people it really belonged to.'

Luna stared at Felix Dashwood. She could sense the fear inside her, yes, but this girl was strong. Her anger overrode all other emotions and made the white smoke around her spark. She would be a difficult one to control if Luna ever needed to.

'You think that is a treasure map?' Now a smile formed on Traiton's face. 'It isn't treasure I am after this time, I can assure you.'

'Then what's the map for?' asked the idiot boy.

Traiton let go of the boy and walked over to his desk. The boy stepped forwards, as if thinking of trying to escape. Luna glared at him and he froze.

Traiton brushed a hand over the map on the desk, a bit too dramatically in Luna's opinion. 'You will find out soon enough what this is for.'

'You've been using everyone at Stormy Cliff, haven't you?' said the girl.

'My, you have been snooping around. Yes, they have been doing some very useful research.'

Luna frowned. What was Traiton doing? He was dangerously close to giving away the plan.

'What have you done to Caspar and Mr Tweedale? Are you blackmailing them to help you?' asked the girl.

'Oh, I don't need to do that. Because I have Luna Claw.'

Luna fixed her eyes on the two children.

Traiton continued, 'Luna has some very special skills.'

Luna turned to Traiton and shook her head, warning him not to say anything else.

The girl turned to her. 'You're controlling them. Hypnotising them or something? How?'

Luna felt her own anger building. She wasn't sure whether to direct it at the girl or Traiton. How dare he give all this away?

When Luna didn't respond, the girl turned back to Traiton. 'If you're not trying to get treasure, then what are you after? I thought you were only interested in money.'

'Oh, there is something far better than money that I am going to get,' Traiton replied evenly with a smile.

'What?' asked the boy.

'I think you have told them enough,' Luna snapped at Traiton.

He ignored her and continued to smile at the children.

'We're going to get off this ship!' the girl yelled then, making the white smoke around her spark and tighten its grip. 'We'll tell everyone you're back on Thistlewick.'

Luna's only hope now was that Traiton would let her take over their minds when he sent them down to the cells. He had told them so much, she needed to wipe their minds to keep the plan safe.

Traiton held his hand out towards the cabin door. 'You are free to leave.'

'What?' Luna couldn't help letting out.

'And you can tell anyone you like about me. Very soon, no one will believe you.' Traiton walked over to the door, opened it and called, 'Come and free the girl from your smoke, Wrigglesworth.'

Luna gripped hold of his arm and spat, 'What are you doing? This is not part of the plan!'

He looked at her, his eyes black. 'Silence.'

Wrigglesworth soared into the cabin and bowed to Traiton, then went over to the girl. He held out his hands and waved them back and forth, muttering to himself, until the smoke had curled away from the girl and shot into a bottle, which he placed in his pocket.

Luna watched, speechless, as Traiton walked Felix Dashwood and Drift Castle out of the cabin.

24

What Next?

Felix and Drift stopped running once they were out of the forest and in South Thistlewick again.

'Why … did Traiton … let us go?' Drift asked between gasps for breath.

Felix blinked several times, trying to ease the confusion in her mind. 'I don't know. He sounded even more evil than I remembered.'

'Luna Claw gave me the creeps too,' said Drift.

'Yeah, it felt like her eyes were burning into my mind.'

'And Caspar's being controlled by her.'

'Poor Caspar. But we still don't know what Traiton is up to.'

'He said that very soon no one will believe us if we tell them he's here.'

'Maybe that means they're planning to control everyone on Thistlewick. Very soon…' Felix stared up at the silvery crescent moon and mulled those words over. She gasped. 'It's Mayor Merryweather and Miss Sugarplume's wedding tomorrow afternoon. Most of Thistlewick will be there. Hundreds of people!'

'Yes! If Traiton and Luna Claw are going to try and take control of everyone, that's when they'll do it, isn't it?'

Felix nodded. 'And then they'll have hundreds of people to use for whatever their evil plan is. If we stand any chance of stopping them, we need to figure out how Luna Claw is controlling Caspar and Mr Tweedale, and how she's going to try to control everyone else.'

She looked at her watch. It was well past nine.

'We'd better get home. We need to act as normally as possible. I'm meant to be at Mrs Didsbury's tomorrow morning. She's told me her house needs a good clean.' Felix groaned. 'All those dog hairs…'

'Can't you just not go?'

'I'll be in way more trouble if I don't. Mrs Didsbury would probably get Mum to lock me in my room, or something. I'll be as quick as I can, then we can figure out what to do next.'

25

Revenge

Luna was still standing, open-mouthed, in Traiton's cabin when he walked back in.

The smile disappeared from his face. 'Do not question me like that again, not in front of the girl.'

'You let them go!' Luna yelled. 'I could have controlled them – wiped their memories!'

'No.'

Continuing to stare at Traiton, Luna unclenched her left fist and thrust her hand towards the shelf behind her. One of the bottles floated upwards, then shot towards Traiton like a bullet. He stepped to the side and the bottle smashed against the wall, sending a blue liquid oozing out.

Wrigglesworth, who had been hovering to one side, disappeared through the opposite wall.

Luna gave a piercing shriek and ten more bottles lifted off the shelf. Together, they fired at Traiton, each one aiming for a different part of his body.

He held his arms up to his face and ducked down, but Luna simply made the bottles change direction towards him. A centimetre away from their target, she closed her left hand and the bottles froze in mid-air.

'You have risked everything by letting them go!' she whispered hoarsely. 'If we are discovered, then you will not be able to take your revenge and neither will I! I will never forgive you for that – and you know what I do to people I don't forgive!'

'It was always my plan to let them go,' said Traiton, hands still covering his face.

Luna opened her left palm and the bottles continued their journey, only just avoiding Traiton and smashing on the wall around him. Various liquids and gases were released into the room, causing a hideous smell of rotten eggs and death.

'From now on, I need to know everything. If you want me to help with your plan, you will not hide anything from me. Yes?'

'Yes,' Traiton replied through gritted teeth. He threw open the cabin door and gasped for clean air.

'Why did you tell the girl so much?'

'Because I want her to be fully aware that I am

about to make something bad happen on Thistlewick. I want her to know that this time there is nothing she can do to stop me. And there isn't, is there? Not with Wrigglesworth's inventions and the powers you possess. When she realises that, and sees my plan take effect, then I will have had my revenge on her.'

He started to walk out of the cabin, but turned back to Luna. 'You must not waste any more thoughts on Felix Dashwood. She is for me to think about. You need to focus all your powers on the big event.'

Luna glared at him, still furious, but nodded.

'Wrigglesworth!' Traiton called.

The ghost's pallid face appeared through the wall again, looking uneasy. 'Has she stopping throwing things now?'

'Yes.'

Wrigglesworth's whole body floated into the cabin to face Traiton. 'I have experimented on the samples that Thomas Tweedale provided, sir.'

'And?' asked Traiton.

'If the rest of the buildings are made of the same material, your plan will be more successful than you had hoped.'

'Excellent. And what about your latest invention?'

'I am still working on it, sir, but it will be ready.'

'Good. I want my revenge to have an explosive ending!'

26

The Crystal Ball

'Get off!' said Felix, trying to pull the brush out of the dog's mouth.

Its teeth were firmly gripped around the middle of the brush. Felix managed to get her hands on either side and tugged.

'Give it here!'

'What is going on?' Mrs Didsbury hobbled into the living room, waving her walking stick.

The dog instantly let go of the brush, sending Felix flying backwards into the dustpan full of dogs' hair, which scattered all over the floor she'd just cleaned.

'Why have you been winding my dogs up?' Mrs Didsbury tutted and glared at her. 'Honestly, look at the mess you have made. Clean it up, this instant.'

Felix sighed. 'Yes, Mrs Didsbury.'

The old lady left the room. Felix quickly gathered

up the dog hair and took it over to the bin. She felt a pull on the leg of her jeans and turned to see another dog standing there expectantly, its tail banging against the hole in the carpet. She realised she was right next to the dogs' cupboard.

'No, dog.'

The dog gave a slight whimper.

'Fine.' Felix looked around to see if Mrs Didsbury was nearby. 'I'm sure she won't mind, if it'll stop you from messing around.

Felix opened up the cupboard door and looked along the single shelf. She saw nothing but a thick layer of dust.

'Sorry, dog, there's nothing here for you.' She looked at the other three in the basket. 'That goes for all of you.'

The dog by her feet padded sulkily back over to join the others.

Felix was about to close the cupboard door when her eyes were once again drawn to the painting at the back. But no, it wasn't a painting – looking closer, Felix could see it was a poster. She nearly jumped backwards when she realised it was Luna Claw!

Felix frowned. Wait, no – this woman had the same wavy hair, blue shawl and golden jewellery, but her face wasn't the same as the woman on the ship. In yellow letters at the top of the poster it advertised: 'Witness the Spectacular Seraphina – the world's most famous fortune-teller!'

Why does Mrs Didsbury have a poster of the Spectacular Seraphina? Felix wondered.

She looked back at the poster – at the woman hunched over a crystal ball.

'What are you doing?'

Felix froze. She turned slowly to see the sharp, wrinkled face of Mrs Didsbury glaring at her.

'Sorry, Mrs Didsbury, I was just…'

'You have no right to go prying in my cupboards.'

'Sorry,' Felix said again. She noticed the old lady's eyes, which were suddenly familiar. She looked back to the poster, but Mrs Didsbury shut the cupboard door.

'What is your first name, Mrs Didsbury?'

'That is none of your business.'

'Is it Seraphina?'

The woman in the poster looked a lot younger, but the more Felix stared at Mrs Didsbury, the more she began to see past her wrinkles. Felix waited, but Mrs Didsbury said nothing.

'Are you the Spectacular Seraphina?'

Mrs Didsbury sighed, the harshness in her face replaced by a pained look. 'That is something I do not talk about, especially not with criminals.'

'But you're famous! You're the world's greatest fortune-teller.'

'I was, yes. But I left it all behind years ago.'

'Why are you on Thistlewick now? Why aren't you living in a big mansion somewhere?'

'I grew up here,' Mrs Didsbury explained. 'I never told anyone when I left to join the circus as a teenager, and I told hardly anyone what I got up to in the years I was away. Only Mayor Merryweather knows, and now … you. You must promise not to tell anyone.'

Once again, Mrs Didsbury's eyes pierced Felix's.

'Why?'

'Just promise!'

'Yes, Mrs Didsbury.' Something occurred to Felix then. 'Do you know someone called Luna Claw?'

'Luna… How did you…?' The change in Mrs Didsbury's expression was instant. She faltered and her eyes widened fearfully. 'No. No more of this. You will finish cleaning the living room, then the hallway and my bedroom.'

Mrs Didsbury started to walk shakily into the kitchen, but turned back round.

'And do not go in the dogs' cupboard again. Don't pry in any of my things – you do not need to open cupboards to clean.'

***

It seemed to take an age to clean the living room and the hallway. But it had given Felix time to think.

It was so strange that Mrs Didsbury – the grumpy, strict old lady – was also the world famous fortune-teller, the Spectacular Seraphina. But Felix felt sure now, from the way Mrs Didsbury had changed when she mentioned Luna Claw, that the old lady knew her – feared her.

Luna Claw looked much younger than Mrs Didsbury was now, but she wore the same outfit that Mrs Didsbury had on in the poster. So Luna must also be a fortune-teller. Felix remembered seeing Luna Claw for the first time – hunched over something on the table; that something must have been a crystal ball, and she was using it somehow to control Mr Tweedale and Caspar!

These thoughts buzzed around Felix's mind as she entered Mrs Didsbury's bedroom, holding a feather duster.

She looked around. It was like the living room – drab and grey. A blackened oak wardrobe, a chest of drawers with a cracked mirror over it, a simple bed with grey sheets and a bedside cabinet.

Felix squinted at the cabinet.

Mrs Didsbury had said not to look inside anything. Felix knew she shouldn't really pry, but was the old lady hiding anything else?

Felix pulled open the cabinet door. A pile of magazines fell out. She shoved them back in, about to shut the door again when she noticed a faint glow coming from under them. She pulled the magazines back out and reached in. She felt something smooth and cold. It was round – about the size of a football.

Felix's mouth fell open. Was this Mrs Didsbury's crystal ball?

She wrapped her hands around it and lifted it out, surprised by how heavy it was. Holding it up carefully in front of her, it looked just like in the poster, and a silvery, smoky substance seemed to shimmer inside it.

Was it with a ball like this that Luna Claw controlled Caspar?

Felix looked at the alarm clock on the bedside cabinet – 11.30, only a couple of hours before the mayor's wedding. She had to show Drift the crystal ball. She took off her jumper and wrapped the ball inside it. Then she walked out of Mrs Didsbury's bedroom and crept down the stairs. She looked around; Mrs Didsbury wasn't in sight. Felix went quickly to her bag in the entrance hall, unzipped it, and placed the crystal ball inside.

'I've finished your bedroom, Mrs Didsbury, so I'm just going out for some lunch.'

'I suppose that is allowed,' the old lady's voice came from the kitchen. 'Do not forget that you are going to look after my dogs while I am at the wedding this afternoon. Be back here to collect them by one o'clock.'

'OK.'

Felix slipped out through the front door.

27

Archibald
von
Hatful

SIXTY YEARS AGO

Luna sat in her caravan outside the circus tent, preparing for her evening performance at the McVegas Circus. As she applied her make-up, she asked her assistant and understudy, Seraphina, to fetch her a drink.

'Of course, Miss Claw.'

A minute later Seraphina returned with a glass of iced lime juice. Luna drank it while polishing her crystal ball. She didn't usually get nervous, but tonight she felt a few butterflies. She had heard rumours that the great showman, Archibald von Hatful, would be paying a visit to the McVegas Circus. He had spent the last year searching for acts to tour the world with him.

As Luna finished her drink, she began to feel light-headed. She put it down to nerves and continued polishing her crystal ball. But as she looked down at it, there were two balls – she was seeing double. They began to spin around and the caravan got darker and darker until Luna was in blackness…

The next thing Luna knew, she was gasping awake.

'Thank goodness,' said Seraphina, sitting at the end of Luna's bed.

'Why am I in bed?' asked Luna, searching for her clock.

'We were really worried. You fainted.'

'Is it time for my performance yet?'

Seraphina looked at her with concerned eyes and a faint smile. 'You have been out cold for hours, Miss Claw. I am afraid I had to go on for you.'

'You what?' Luna sat up.

'I am your understudy, after all.'

'Did von Hatful come?'

'No,' Seraphina replied.

'You're lying.'

'I'm not, I swear. Now, I said I would go and meet someone. I promise I will come back soon to check on you. You must rest.'

With that, Seraphina got up and left. Luna tried to move – to get out of bed – but her head was heavy and she fell back against the pillow.

The next morning, when Luna woke, she could move again, but when she went to Seraphina's caravan there was no one inside. None of the others around the circus had seen her.

Luna stormed into the small tent Colin McVegas used as an office.

'Where is Seraphina?' she demanded.

McVegas looked up from his desk and grimaced. 'You aren't going to like what I am about to tell you, my dear.'

'Was von Hatful in last night?'

'Yes … and, when you were taken ill, Seraphina took your place in the performance.'

Luna clenched her fists. 'She lied. I knew it. She's gone off with him, hasn't she?'

McVegas shrank down in his chair guiltily. 'He was impressed with her performance. So impressed that he asked her to join his world tour. She left on his boat straight away.'

Luna leant across the desk, grabbed his collar and pulled him up to face her. 'I haven't been ill for five years. She poisoned me, didn't she?'

'What are you talking about, Luna?' He pulled himself away.

'She gave me poisoned lime juice last night, so that while I was out cold she could take my place.'

'My dear, you are being a tad rash. Seraphina filled your glass up from my personal supply of fresh lime juice. I squeezed it myself yesterday morning.'

'Then she must have added poison after she filled the glass up.'

McVegas tried to pat her arm, but she batted him away.

He sighed. 'I know you must be furious. It would have been a marvellous opportunity and you would have impressed Mr von Hatful even more than Seraphina, I am sure. But it is she who he saw, not you, and we must put it down to bad luck that you were ill last night. At any rate, I count myself lucky that I get to keep you here in my circus. You are a wonderful performer, Luna.'

'Aaarrrggghhh!' Feeling a boiling rage she had never before experienced, Luna stormed out of his tent.

28

Playing Chicken

'That's what Luna Claw uses to control people?' Drift stared at the ball in Felix's hand.

They were standing on Primpit Lane, its quaint cottages reflected in the ball.

'One like it, yes. This is Mrs Didsbury's.'

'I still don't believe that Mrs Didsbury was a world-famous fortune-teller. Go on, try reading my future.'

'We don't have time, Drift. If Luna is using her crystal ball to control Caspar and Mr Tweedale, we need to figure out how it works.'

'How are we going to do that?'

'Let's see if I can control you. Stand still,' Felix ordered.

Drift gave her a mock solute and stood in front of her. Felix held up the crystal ball with both hands and could see him reflected in the silvery smoke inside it.

'I want to control Drift,' she spoke into it. 'I want to get into his mind and control him.'

She waited. Nothing changed.

'Er … I'm not feeling controlled,' said Drift.

'No, it can't be that simple.'

Felix thought back to seeing Luna through the black curtain. She had been hunched over her crystal ball, but she hadn't been saying anything.

'Maybe I need to think it, rather than saying it.'

She stared into the crystal ball and thought, *Drift. Drift. Drift!*

Her fingers tingled as tiny blue sparks came off the crystal ball.

'I think it's working.'

She stared into the ball and focused on the reflection of Drift.

Go into Drift's mind and control him. The ball sparked even more. She tried to make her thoughts as loud as possible. *Go on! Into his mind!*

The image in the crystal ball changed. The smoke cleared and now she wasn't just looking at Drift's reflection – the image had zoomed in so that Drift's head now filled the whole ball.

'Drift?' she asked.

There was no reply. She looked up from the crystal ball and saw Drift's body tense and his arms flop down by his side. He stared ahead with dead eyes – just like Mr Tweedale's and Caspar's.

She looked back to the crystal ball and considered what to make Drift do. *Make him walk around like a chicken.*

A sound came out of his mouth that made Felix jump. 'Bwak! Bwak! *Bwak!'*

Drift was squawking like a chicken! He folded his hands into his armpits and moved his arms up and down like wings. Felix burst out laughing. He knelt down, thrust his head forwards and pecked at the grass with his nose.

OK, you can stop now!

She looked up from the crystal ball.

Drift frowned at her from the ground. 'What happened?'

'Oh, nothing,' said Felix, giggling. 'I just made you walk around a bit. Don't you remember?'

'No, not really.'

Felix's delight was quickly replaced by anger and concern. 'This is definitely how Luna Claw is controlling Caspar and Mr Tweedale.'

'But *The Relampagos* is in North Thistlewick. She must be able to use it over a long distance,' said Drift.

'So let's see if I can do that. Hide round the corner and I'll try to control you.'

'OK.' Drift fumbled around in his bag and handed something to Felix. 'It's a walkie-talkie. I've got one too. You can press the button on the side to speak to me.'

He walked off and disappeared out of sight. A minute later, Felix's walkie-talkie crackled.

'I'm standing on Rough Hill Lane,' came Drift's voice.

Felix looked into the crystal ball and, of course, couldn't see Drift – just the reflection of what was directly in front of her.

Find Drift, she thought.

Nothing changed.

He's on Rough Hill Lane.

Nothing.

'Hmmm…' she muttered.

She looked deep into the crystal ball and tried to really focus her mind, shutting out all other thoughts and just thinking about Drift standing on Rough Hill Lane.

An image of the lane formed in her mind, with its block of flats on one side and cramped cottages on the other. Her hands buzzed and she felt sparks from the crystal ball wrap around her fingers. The image inside the crystal ball clouded and changed to match the one in her mind. And standing there in the middle of the lane was Drift.

Felix smiled, but kept her mind focused on him.

Go inside Drift's mind. The crystal ball zoomed in on his face and his eyes deadened. *Now make him dance like a ballerina!*

She watched as the image zoomed out to show Drift raise himself onto tiptoes and lift his arms high in the air. He spun delicately around and around. Mrs Spindle came out of the block of flats behind Drift. She frowned at him.

You can stop now, Felix told the crystal ball.

Drift flopped back down into his normal slouched pose. He pulled his walkie-talkie out.

'Hey,' he said into it, 'why is Mrs Spindle staring at me oddly? What did you make me do?'

'Nothing,' Felix replied. 'But you'd look good in a tutu.'

They continued to experiment with the crystal ball. Drift kept moving further away from Felix. She then pictured where he was in her mind and he appeared in the crystal ball for her to control. The further away he got, though, the harder Felix had to focus to get the image of the place to appear in the ball. It was giving her a headache.

'OK, I'm down at the harbour now,' Drift's voice came through the walkie-talkie.

This was an easy image for Felix to picture. She knew the harbour well. Soon she felt the familiar tingling against her fingers ... followed by a sharp pain, like an electric shock. She pulled her hand back and nearly dropped the crystal ball.

Inside it the harbour was appearing, but it was faint and clouded in smoke.

Felix tried to ignore the buzzing at her fingers and focused as hard as she could on the image of the harbour. But it didn't get any clearer.

She pulled out her walkie-talkie. 'No good, Drift. I think you've gone too far.'

***

'The last time you were able to control me I was on Stowaway Lane,' said Drift when they met up at the market. 'According to my map, that's two kilometres away from where you were standing.'

'That's how far away the crystal ball can be used from, then.'

Drift nodded and held out his map. 'And look, the distance between the church and the cove *The Relampagos* is hiding in is just under two kilometres.'

'So Luna Claw is almost as far away as she can be to control everyone at the wedding,' said Felix.

She looked up at the sound of whistling. It was Farmer Potts walking past them. He wore his usual rough, chequered shirt, but today had a tie around his neck.

'Oh no, people are going to the wedding already. I'm meant to be looking after Mrs Didsbury's dogs.'

'What's the plan, then?' asked Drift. 'We know that Luna Claw is going to use a crystal ball to control everyone, but how are we going to stop her?'

'I don't know. You need to go to the church. Keep an eye on what's going on and walkie-talkie me.'

'What are you going to do?'

'I'm going to collect the dogs, then go back up to *The Relampagos*. I can use Mrs Didsbury's crystal ball to see what's happening on the ship.'

'Alright, but be careful,' said Drift.

29

The Spectacular Seraphina

Luna stared out of her cabin window, thinking back to *that* night sixty years ago. The night when nothing changed, but when everything should have changed.

Seraphina had stolen Luna's chance at fame and fortune.

In the months that followed, Luna continued to perform to the handfuls of people who came to the McVegas Circus. As the circus toured around England's poorest villages, she followed Seraphina Didsbury's career in the papers and on the radio. The 'Spectacular Seraphina', von Hatful had decided to call her. Luna had read with bitterness about her performance to the president of the United States, about her nightly audiences of over ten thousand people. Crowds flocked to see Seraphina arriving on her million pound yacht, while Luna travelled in a leaky caravan. She should have been on that yacht – she should have been the famous one.

Luna thought back to the time when she had really exploded – when she was reading about Seraphina's performance to the Queen of England. At that very moment Luna came up with her plan of revenge. Luna would let Seraphina lead the life that she should have had, and then Luna would pounce.

She started to take potions and learn spells to keep herself young, and continued in Colin McVegas's circus. Fifty years had gone by when Seraphina announced her farewell world tour. This would be the perfect time for Luna to take her revenge and she booked herself a ticket to see the 'Spectacular Seraphina' perform in London.

But the night before the performance, it was cancelled. Seraphina had disappeared and no one knew where she had gone. Luna had tortured Archibald von Hatful to get him to tell her, but not even he had known. Seraphina Didsbury must have suspected that Luna was after her, and she had fled.

It was ten years later that Luna had received the message from Tristan Traiton, offering her the opportunity she could not refuse.

Now Luna was ready to take what should have been hers in the first place. Seraphina's memories. That would be her revenge. They were a treasure greater than any gold or diamond. Once Luna had helped Traiton, she would extract those memories, painfully slowly, from Seraphina. Then she would breathe all the memories in – she would live the life that Seraphina had had and grow old with her memories. And Seraphina Didsbury would be left with nothing.

Luna smiled as she looked down at her crystal ball. Not long now. This afternoon, Traiton would have his revenge and this evening, Luna would have hers.

Into Luna's Mind

Felix peeked out from behind the bush. *The Relampagos* was still hidden in the cove below. No one was on deck. She took out her walkie-talkie and pressed the button on the side.

'Drift? Can you hear me?'

There was a short pause, then a buzzing sound that sounded like lots of people chattering.

'Yep,' said Drift.

'How are things going at the church?'

'Everyone is just heading in. There are loads of people. It'll be crammed. Mr Tweedale's here with about half the class, but Caspar hasn't turned up.'

Another voice came faintly over the walkie-talkie. 'Drift, what are you doing?'

'Sorry, Felix, Dad's calling me in. The wedding's about to start,' said Drift.

'OK. Keep an eye on Mr Tweedale and let me know if anything happens.'

The buzzing noise stopped and Felix put the walkie-talkie in her pocket. She walked back along the edge of the forest until she came to the tree she had tied Mrs Didsbury's dogs to. They all jumped up at her, their tails wagging so fast she thought they might drop off.

'Down, dogs,' she said.

She lifted the crystal ball out of her backpack and stared closely at it. The smoke inside it sparkled and she felt its warm glow.

She shut all her other thoughts out and tried to picture Luna's cabin on *The Relampagos* – the woman sitting at the desk surrounded by vibrant blue colours.

Show me Luna Claw's cabin.

The smoke in the crystal ball slowly swirled around. Her fingers tingled and Luna appeared in the ball. Felix saw her from behind, like she had when she'd peeked through the black curtain, hunched over the table.

Now, take me into Luna's mind.

The image in the crystal ball began to zoom in. Felix held her breath as she grew closer and closer to the back of Luna's head.

31

The Wedding Begins

Through her crystal ball, Luna watched the last few people enter the church.

She glared at Seraphina Didsbury sitting near the front. She saw Drift Castle in the middle of the congregation. The girl was nowhere to be seen – she was probably hiding somewhere – but the place was certainly packed, with every seat taken and many other people standing at the back.

The mayor, dressed in a pompous purple suit, stood with the vicar at the front, and Thomas Tweedale and the choir sat in pews nearby.

Luna nodded confidently – everything was ready.

An organ started playing and everyone stood. Luna

felt the music echoing around her head as it would be in the church. She watched with mild disgust as April Sugarplume slowly walked up the aisle, wearing a long white gown with colourful flowers draped over it.

When she reached the front, the congregation sat and the vicar began, 'We are gathered here today to witness the wedding of Mayor Roderick Merryweather and Miss April Sugarplume.'

Luna rolled her eyes as April looked towards the mayor with a beaming smile. The sooner they got to the song, the better.

Two sparks rose up through the crystal ball then, shooting into Luna's hands. She blinked in shock – and when she looked back at the ball the image of the church had gone, replaced by a staticky whiteness.

Luna felt her mind growing heavy, like something was interfering with it – like someone was trying to control *her*. She gasped. No, that wasn't possible. Seraphina Didsbury was at the church, and she was the only other person with the means to control people. Anyway, Seraphina didn't know that Luna was there.

She focused her mind and forced the feeling out. The ship was so far away from the church that her crystal ball had probably just lost connection and bounced all her controlling thoughts back at her.

Luna thought hard about the church once more, and an image of the place reappeared in the ball, faint and flickering.

The curtain swept open behind her and Traiton appeared.

'Everything OK?' he asked.

For once his arrival was welcome. 'We are too far away. My crystal ball is losing connection with the church, and without that connection I have no control. Sail the ship back to the south, Traiton, nearer the church.'

North

Felix breathed deeply in and out, trying to recover from the shock.

'I'm not trying that again,' she said to the dogs, which had stopped messing around and were looking at her curiously. When she'd used the crystal ball to focus on Luna's mind, it had worked for a moment before she'd been pushed out, and two lightning bolts had shot up from the ball into her body, shaking her to the core.

So Luna could push Felix out of her mind. But there had to be another way to stop her.

Felix tentatively touched the crystal ball and felt relieved when it didn't try to electrocute her. This time, she focused all her thoughts on an image of *The Relampagos* as a whole.

The full length of the ship appeared in the ball. She saw Traiton on the deck, unfurling one of the sails. The thin, weedy ghost, Wrigglesworth, was at the wheel. Felix started. *The Relampagos* was moving out of the cove, sailing south!

They were moving it nearer to the church. That would make Luna's connection stronger!

Felix remembered how weak her connection had been earlier with the harbour and it gave her an idea – if she could find a way to make the ship steer the other way, north, she could break the connection between Luna's crystal ball and the church.

She stared into the crystal ball and tried desperately to think how she could do it. She focused on Wrigglesworth at the wheel. If she could get into his mind, then she might be able to make him steer the ship the other way. But was it even possible to control a ghost's mind?

Felix gripped hold of the crystal ball and thought, *Zoom in on the wheel.*

Now she was looking at the top of Wrigglesworth's partially see-through head.

Enter Wrigglesworth's mind.

Her fingers vibrated as the crystal ball followed her orders. Her body tensed and she half expected the ball to electrocute her, like it had moments before. But Wrigglesworth didn't show any resistance like Luna had. His eyes went dead and his head swung backwards, as if he was in a trance. Wrigglesworth was under Felix's control.

She took a breath and thought, *Turn the ship around, Wrigglesworth. Head north, not south!*

33

The Choir

Go ahead, Thomas Tweedale, Luna thought. *Through you, I will take control of everyone.*

In the church, the head teacher raised his left arm up, brought it down, and the Stormy Cliff choir began to sing.

'It's a wedding day, it's a happy day
For all of us to share
On our island, we walk hand in hand
When love is in the air.'

Luna fought to hold back a sickly feeling as the words, written by April Sugarplume, rang around her head. She focused her mind on Thomas Tweedale and, through his arm movements, started to control the choir. Their singing took on a hypnotic quality, rising high, then low, then high.

As the first verse came to an end, Luna looked around the church and saw that the singing was starting to have an effect. The congregation were all fully awake, but their eyes were fixed on the choir.

Louder and stronger, Luna thought.

She made Thomas Tweedale's hand strokes larger and more forceful and the choir responded.

'In the summertime, when the weather is … fine
And flow … ers dance around …'

Luna frowned as the image in her crystal ball flickered again. Her connection with the church was getting weaker, not stronger – and just at the wrong time!

She grabbed the ball and stormed out of her cabin. Up on deck she saw the ship was pointed north.

'You're sailing the wrong way!' she yelled. 'Why are you heading north?'

'I don't know,' Traiton called from the quarterdeck. He was staring at Wrigglesworth and seemed just as baffled as Luna. 'Wrigglesworth, what are you doing, man? Turn us back around!'

Luna strode up the steps to join them and recognised the dead look in Wrigglesworth's eyes.

'He ... he's being controlled.'

'You're controlling him?' asked Traiton.

'No.'

'Then who?'

Luna looked into her crystal ball and through the flickering image she saw Seraphina still sitting in the church, and Drift Castle too. Felix Dashwood was still not there.

It must be the girl. But how could she have figured out how to control Wrigglesworth? Did she have Seraphina's crystal ball? Luna cursed herself for getting Felix Dashwood sent to Seraphina's house.

'It's the girl – I think she has another crystal ball,' Luna snarled at Traiton. 'You should not have told her so much.'

Traiton looked from Wrigglesworth to Luna and bit his lip, his eyebrows forming a deep, uncertain frown. Then, slowly, his mouth curled into a smile.

'No, this will only make my revenge sweeter – when she realises that no matter what she does, she cannot stop us.'

He swung his hand towards Wrigglesworth and heaved the ghost away from the wheel. Wrigglesworth floated nearby, motionless.

'You useless, weedy excuse for a ghost!' Traiton spat at him. He began turning the ship around. 'Felix Dashwood will not get into my mind. You can stop her, yes?'

Luna looked back at her crystal ball. The image of the church was growing stronger again. 'No, I am at a crucial point in the plan here. If you want your revenge, I need to focus on the church. You figure out how to deal with the girl.'

She swung around and walked down the steps. She heard Traiton yelling at Wrigglesworth, telling him to take his dog, find Felix Dashwood and do whatever it took to stop her.

Luna glanced up as the ghosts soared away, and saw that Traiton was now steering the ship south.

When she sat down in her cabin, she focused her mind completely on the church within her crystal ball, and on Thomas Tweedale conducting the choir. Now, when she looked at the people listening to the singing, she could see their eyes deadening. Her control was taking full effect.

The Singing

'Come on!'

Felix stared in frustration at the crystal ball. No matter how hard she tried, Traiton wasn't letting her into his mind. He was angry, and somehow his rage was blocking her.

Now Luna had figured out that Felix was using a crystal ball too, Felix was definitely in trouble. She had lost control of Wrigglesworth when Traiton sent him to find her, and it probably wouldn't be long before the ghost turned up.

Felix pulled out her walkie-talkie. 'What's happening at the church, Drift?'

For about thirty seconds there was no reply.

'Drift?'

Still no response.

Finally, a noise came through. At first it was the

sound of muffled singing, then Drift's voice. 'Sorry, I kind of zoned out.'

'Is that the Stormy Cliff choir I can hear singing?' asked Felix.

'Yeah.'

'Look around you, Drift. Is everyone else zoned out too?'

She waited anxiously, and a few seconds later the reply came back, 'They're all looking blankly ahead, like Caspar and Mr Tweedale. Hang on. Dad? Dad?' The sound cut out for a second, then returned. 'I just tried talking to Dad. He didn't even notice me tugging his arm.'

'Then it's the singing! Luna Claw is using the singing to get control of everyone.'

'Of course!' said Drift. 'Why didn't we think of that before? But no one's doing anything – they're all just sitting there, like they're sleeping with their eyes open.'

Felix heard a low rumble nearby and looked up. Ten metres away was the ghost dog from the ship.

'You … you have to do something to stop the choir, Drift!' she managed to get out, and then she lowered the walkie-talkie.

The dog edged towards her, growling aggressively, its fur sticking out, its razor-teeth bared.

Felix backed away, but the dog just kept on coming.

35

Interruption

'And it's on a wedding day that we all say…'

With each word of the song the people in the church fell further and further under Luna's control. Next to the choir, Mayor Merryweather and April Sugarplume were arm-in-arm, rocking from side to side.

Luna looked at the congregation, all sitting there with their eyes glazed over. She could do anything she wanted to them, but that wasn't part of the plan. She just had to get them to drift into a deeper and deeper sleep.

Luna's thoughts were cut off by someone yelling. She scanned around the congregation, until she saw Drift Castle stand up and jump up and down. He waved his hands in front of people's faces and pushed his way through them towards the choir, shouting all the way.

The boy stood in front of Thomas Tweedale and tried to conduct the choir himself.

Idiot boy! thought Luna.

An idiot he might be, but she could feel her control slipping as the singing was broken up by his noise.

She focused on Thomas Tweedale. *Get two of the children to remove him from the church!*

Tweedale continued conducting with one hand, but with the other he pointed at two of the children and then at Drift. The children nodded and broke away from the choir. They walked towards Drift, who backed away, but the two children grabbed him. Although the boy kicked and squirmed, through Luna's power the children had far more strength than normal.

Take him out! Tie him up outside, she thought.

Thomas Tweedale waved a hand towards the church door. The children dragged Drift Castle down the central aisle of the church, while the boy screamed out, 'Don't let them control you! Don't listen to the song! Put your fingers in your ears!'

A few people turned to look at him, but most were too far into their sleep-state.

Once Drift Castle was out through the door, Luna looked back at the congregation. They were still under her control. Yes, it was time to move on to the second part of the plan.

Continue the singing, she told Thomas Tweedale.

Then she thought about where Caspar Littlepage and the other children were. *Tumbledown House.*

She pictured it in her mind and the image of Caspar and five other children standing outside the house appeared in the crystal ball. The six of them had fallen most fully under her control these past few days, and she could get them to do anything.

Time to start burning, she told Caspar.

'Rocco, light the match,' said Caspar.

Rocco walked over to Skye, who was holding a giant match – about a metre long. It would have needed a huge matchbox to strike it against, but this was one of Wrigglesworth's inventions, so it was easier than that. Rocco breathed on the end of the match and it instantly burst into flame.

Skye and Rocco held the match up to a wooden beam of Tumbledown House. The beam glowed orange, then red and the fire quickly spread up it.

The further the flames went, the faster they got, until they were shooting around the wooden frame of the house like a rocket. The flames found the beam of wood that connected the house to the one next to it and that caught fire too.

Luna's eyes glowed from the brightness of what she was seeing in her crystal ball.

Excellent! she thought. *Now, move on to the market – to the newsagent's!*

36

Attack

Holding the crystal ball tightly, Felix backed into the tree Mrs Didsbury's dogs were tied to. She froze as the ghost dog came nearer, its huge mouth slobbering aggressively.

The four dogs around her were like mice compared to it, but they growled nonetheless and pulled on their leads. The ghost dog stopped and tilted its glowing blue head at them. Then one of Mrs Didsbury's dogs barked. The others joined in – sharp piercing yaps. The ghost dog's fur flattened, making it seem much thinner, and it backed away, whimpering. Felix let out a breath. It was obviously all growl and no bite!

Felix moved a safe distance away and watched Mrs Didsbury's dogs continue to tug on their leads, trying to get at the strange see-through creature in front of them.

'There you are!' a voice cried.

Felix turned to see Wrigglesworth soaring along the

treeline towards her. He twisted his face into a snarl.

'Let go of your crystal ball, this instant,' said Wrigglesworth. 'Give it to me.'

'Why should I?'

'I'm warning you. Give me the ball, or…'

'Or what? You'll set your dog on me? He doesn't look that scary any more.' She pointed at the ghost dog, now cowering behind a tree as Mrs Didsbury's dogs growled at it. 'Or will you try to haunt me? I've met ghosts far worse than you, Wrigglesworth!'

'But I bet those other ghosts didn't have this.'

He pulled something out of his pocket. Felix squinted – it was hard to see as the sky darkened overhead. He was holding a bottle. Wrigglesworth gave her a toothy grin and, as he uncorked it, she saw something slippery and white – the smoke that had captured her on the ship.

Felix took a step back.

'Ha! Now I've got you worried. Place the crystal ball down on the ground, girl.'

Felix ignored him. She held the ball up, the ghost reflected in it. *Take me into Wrigglesworth's mind.*

The crystal ball buzzed and the image inside it zoomed in on Wrigglesworth. The smoke floated in front of him and he whispered to it.

Now take control of hi—

Felix didn't finish the thought. Wrigglesworth opened his arms wide and the smoke shot away from him. Felix held the crystal ball to her chest and dived behind a tree.

She pressed herself against the tree, heart pumping, trying not to breath. The smoke soared past the tree and stopped in mid-air. It seemed to look first left, then right, trying to locate its prey. Suddenly it saw her and fired at the tree. Felix got up and charged back out into the open. When she looked around she saw the smoke passing *through* the tree.

'You can't outrun my smoke, girl. Give up now!' called Wrigglesworth.

Felix turned to face the rapidly approaching smoke. An idea struck her. She fell down onto the ground and curled into a tight ball, pressing the crystal ball against her legs and her head against the ball.

A second later she felt the power of Wrigglesworth's smoke as it wrapped around the outside of her body. It squeezed and cut into her like rope.

Felix gritted her teeth to shut out the pain as the smoke dragged her along the ground. But right in front of her face was the crystal ball. Inside it, she only saw the darkness of her own legs.

She pictured Wrigglesworth floating by the trees and he appeared in the crystal ball.

Enter his mind! The image zoomed into him and the snarl on his face disappeared, replaced by a blank look. *Wrigglesworth, take your smoke away from me and return to* The Relampagos *straight away.*

In the crystal ball, she saw Wrigglesworth raise his arm up and mutter something. Then she felt the smoke around her loosen its grip. As quickly as it had wrapped her up, it freed her. She looked up to see the smoke soaring back into Wrigglesworth's bottle. He replaced the stopper, put it in his pocket, turned around and soared off towards the edge of the cliff.

The ghost dog looked at its disappearing owner. Mrs Didsbury's four snarling dogs blocked its way towards him. With a yelp, it pounded off through the trees and into the forest.

Felix stood up and took several deep breaths.

'Well done,' she told Mrs Didsbury's dogs. She grabbed her walkie-talkie with a shaking hand. 'Drift, what's happening at the church?'

'I don't know,' the reply came. 'I've been dragged outside.'

'Can't you get back in?'

'They've tied me to a gravestone.'

'Oh.'

'Everyone is totally under Luna Claw's control now,' said Drift. 'But, Felix, I don't think Traiton wants to use them for anything.'

'What do you mean?'

'Luna is sending them to sleep – everyone except Caspar and a few others from our class. Traiton just wants everyone out of the way so that he can set fire to the island.'

'What?!' Felix shouted.

'I saw flames coming from the buildings over to the

east a minute ago, and now Caspar and the others have turned up here. They're in the market square opposite me – they're setting fire to your mum's newsagent's!'

37

The Bomb

'We sing out loud, because we are proud
To witness this wedding
Of two people, whose love is full
Symbolised by a ring.'

Luna hummed along as the choir sang.

People around the church were slumped over. Several leant on each other's shoulders, snoring. They wouldn't notice anything that was happening outside the church – which was just as well, because smoke now billowed in from the fire spreading around the market.

As Luna thought about the market, it appeared in her crystal ball in a blaze of red and yellow.

She focused on Caspar.

It is time, she told him. *Head to the cave and get the bomb ready.*

This was the invention Wrigglesworth had died making. A bomb small enough to fit in a pocket, but powerful enough to cause untold damage to the toughest of rock.

'So you are saying that if this bomb works, Stormy Cliff School will be toast?' Traiton had asked Wrigglesworth yesterday.

'Along with most of West Thistlewick, sir,' the ghost had replied, 'including Felix Dashwood's house.'

'Excellent!' Traiton had exclaimed.

Luna sat back, smiled, and watched Caspar giving the other children their orders.

38

All Tied Up

Felix watched *The Relampagos* cutting through the choppy waves in the gloom of dusk.

Now she knew what Traiton had been planning all along: to get Caspar and the others to set fire to the whole of Thistlewick – to destroy all the buildings, including her mum's shop! Felix tried desperately to think of what to do. But there was no time to think – she had to act.

Traiton was steering the ship and she couldn't control him. Luna was in her cabin and Felix couldn't enter her mind either. She spotted Wrigglesworth soaring back onto the ship. He was the only person whose mind Felix had been able to control.

Felix focused on Wrigglesworth's mind.

'Well?' Traiton asked Wrigglesworth.

Tell him you stopped me from using the crystal ball, Felix thought.

'I stopped her from using the crystal ball,' the ghost said in a flat voice.

'Excellent! There's nothing that can get in my way now.' Traiton turned back to the wheel.

Felix raked a hand through her hair. There had to be a way she could use Wrigglesworth to stop Traiton. But the ghost wouldn't have the strength to pull Traiton away from the wheel or fight him – she'd already seen that.

Then Felix remembered the smoke, which must still be in his pocket.

Wrigglesworth, get your smoke out.

He lifted his hand down to the left-hand pocket of his jacket. Felix watched him uncork the bottle and wiggle his fingers like he was conjuring a snake. Out came the stream of smoke. It floated in front of his face, as if waiting for an instruction.

Use the smoke to tie Traiton up, like you tied me up before.

He cupped the smoke in his hands and whispered to it, 'Your target is Tristan Traiton. Tie him to the mast.'

Wrigglesworth opened his hands and the smoke curled away towards Traiton. He was so intent on steering the ship that he didn't notice the white smoky tendrils slithering up his left leg and tying it to his right. It was only when it reached his stomach that he looked down.

'What the…?'

Traiton went to rip the smoke away, but as soon as

he touched it he pulled his hand back, like he had been electrocuted.

Felix allowed herself a smile as the smoke continued to wrap around his body.

He turned to Wrigglesworth. 'What are you doing, man? Get your smoke off me!'

Wrigglesworth stared at him, emotionless.

Traiton let go of the wheel and lunged at the ghost, but, before he got close, the smoke wrapped his arms up behind his back. It pulled him over to the nearest mast and tied him firmly to it.

He struggled against the smoke to no avail. Felix remembered its tight squeeze and knew he would not escape.

Traiton stared at Wrigglesworth, eyebrows raised in shock. 'She's still controlling you, isn't she? You didn't stop her from using the crystal ball, did you?'

He began shouting for help and Felix laughed, but then stopped, realising she needed to move quickly.

She focused on Wrigglesworth. *Take hold of the wheel and turn the ship around again. Head north, and don't let anyone stop you.*

Wrigglesworth took a firm grip on the wheel and spun it round.

Felix's walkie-talkie buzzed and Drift said, 'Felix, are you there?'

'Yep. Traiton's tied up and I'm making Wrigglesworth steer the ship north again.'

'It's no good, Felix,' said Drift, voice high with panic. 'The market's on fire and no one in the church has even realised! And listen!'

There was a muffled noise, then Felix heard Caspar, loud and clear. 'Rocco, do you have the bomb?'

'Yes,' he replied, 'in my pocket.'

'Then we will take it to Burnt Tree Beach,' Caspar ordered them.

'Bomb?!' Felix cried. 'Drift, they're not serious, are they?'

'They're very serious,' said Drift. 'They're going to put it in the cave they were looking in the other day – the one that runs under the whole of West Thistlewick. It'll blow up Stormy Cliff!'

'And my house!'

'Yes. But there's nothing I can do to stop them – I can't get out of this rope. You have to get Luna Claw further away, Felix. You have to break her control before they blow up half of Thistlewick!'

Felix looked back at the crystal ball. *Keep going, Wrigglesworth! Keep heading north! Don't let anything stop you!*

39

Two Crystal Balls

Luna studied the congregation at the church closely. They were all sound asleep.

She thought back to Burnt Tree Beach. Great excitement bubbled inside her as she watched the children arrive there.

Once they got to the cave entrance, they all stopped. Caspar Littlepage frowned at the sand by his feet and the others stood there awkwardly, looking unsure of what to do.

Take the bomb into the cave! Luna thought.

But Caspar didn't move, or make any sign that he had heard her instruction.

Luna focused all her energy on the crystal ball, but

nothing happened. Then the image started to flicker, before disappearing altogether.

'Aaargh!'

She leant back in frustration. As her attention left the crystal ball she heard shouting coming from the deck above. Traiton.

In an instant, she'd climbed up on deck, carrying the crystal ball with her.

Wrigglesworth stood at the wheel again, steering the ship north through a stormy sea, and Traiton was tied to the ship's mast, squirming against Wrigglesworth's smoke.

'I thought you'd dealt with the girl,' said Luna. 'Caspar Littlepage is too far away – I've nearly lost control of him!'

'Wrigglesworth failed to stop Felix Dashwood,' said Traiton. 'She's controlling him again! Can't you get this smoke off me?'

'No,' said Luna. 'It only answers to Wrigglesworth.'

'Then get Wrigglesworth away from the wheel!'

Luna swept over to him. 'Wrigglesworth?'

He didn't respond – of course he didn't. The ghost was weak, and completely lost in the girl's control. Luna placed her hand on his shoulder. A searing pain shot up her arm. Her skin felt like it was on fire. She pulled away.

'He's surrounded himself with more smoke. I can't touch him!'

Traiton's eyes grew wide and mad. 'Luna, do

something! If you can't stop Wrigglesworth, then stop the girl. Can't you control her?'

'I will try.'

Luna looked into her crystal ball. *Find Felix Dashwood.*

A few seconds later, an image of the girl flickered into the ball. Felix was holding Seraphina's crystal ball.

Luna brought her ball to her face. Trying to control someone through another crystal ball was incredibly tricky, but if it worked it had a far more powerful effect. She focused all her energy on the mind of Felix Dashwood.

40

Smash

Felix jumped back as the image of Wrigglesworth in her crystal ball was replaced by Luna Claw's face. Felix stared into her eyes, red and dangerous, like a snake about to attack its prey. Luna's eyebrows arched and she lifted a hand up. As her sharp, claw-like fingernails curled round in the crystal ball, it felt like they were scratching at Felix's mind.

'Aaahhh!' she cried.

Luna's fingers curled around again, digging into Felix. Luna's red lips pursed together in a thin smile.

A rumble of thunder echoed around the sky, followed quickly by a bolt of lightning, which momentarily blinded Felix. She managed to break away from the crystal ball then.

There was another low rumble, but this one came from nearby. She looked for Mrs Didsbury's dogs, but they were all cowering behind their tree, scared by the approaching storm. The rumble came again, directly behind her. She turned to see the ghost dog standing there, its blue outline bristling.

'Dogs, attack!' she said to Mrs Didsbury's dogs.

But there was another flash of lightning and the four of them huddled together.

The ghost dog edged towards Felix, teeth bared. She backed away and the dog leapt in the air, towards her head. She dived to the ground, but the dog pounced.

Felix covered her face with one hand as the dog slobbered down over her. But it didn't bite. It opened its mouth wide and grabbed the crystal ball.

'No!'

The dog began to shake the ball from side to side. With a big swing, it let go, sending the crystal ball flying through the air. With a crunch it hit a tree, smashing into a thousand pieces, which scattered across the ground.

The dog looked back at her, let out a loud bark, then bounded off back towards *The Relampagos*.

Felix's eyes scanned the bits of crystal ball that sparkled in amongst the grass. 'No! No! No!'

There was no hope now. She had lost control of Wrigglesworth and there was no way of stopping Luna Claw.

41

Back in Control

Luna looked up. 'I didn't even need to control the girl. Wrigglesworth's dog just smashed her crystal ball! She can no longer control Wrigglesworth.'

Traiton breathed a long sigh of relief. 'Wrigglesworth! Can you hear me?'

'Y-yes, sir,' the weedy ghost replied, swaying back and forth by the wheel. 'Sorry, sir, I don't know what came over me.'

'For goodness' sake, get your smoke off me!'

Wrigglesworth released the wheel and went over to Traiton. He mumbled something and the smoke started to unwind itself from Traiton and the mast and travel back into the bottle in Wrigglesworth's pocket.

Traiton stumbled away from the mast.

The huge ghost dog soared back onto the ship and landed next to its master.

'Good boy, Stormy, good boy!' said Wrigglesworth, patting its head.

Luna looked down at the crystal ball and thought about Burnt Tree Beach, but no image appeared.

'I haven't quite lost control, but in this weather I need to get much closer to South Thistlewick,' said Luna. 'Then I can tell Caspar Littlepage to place the bomb in the cave and set it to detonate.'

Wrigglesworth's mouth spread into a wide grin. 'My bomb! My most powerful invention! I have been looking forward to this.'

'Then let's get *The Relampagos* down to South Thistlewick.' Traiton grabbed the wheel and, with a huge tug, spun it around. The ship groaned as it fought to turn against the angry waves. 'Will Felix Dashwood be able to see the explosion from where she is, Wrigglesworth?'

'Oh, yes, sir. It will be seen and heard for miles around.'

'But no one else on Thistlewick will even realise,' said Traiton. 'Only Felix Dashwood will see her island being destroyed!'

42

Smoke

'The crystal ball's smashed, Drift,' Felix said quietly into the walkie-talkie.

'Now what do we do?'

'There's nothing we can do. You're tied to a gravestone, watching the market burn down, and I have no way of stopping Traiton.'

'We can't let him beat us.'

'It's over,' said Felix. 'Thistlewick is being destroyed and… Hang on, Drift.'

'Wha—'

Felix released the walkie-talkie button. She stared down at the pieces of crystal ball. Out of the centre of them, a thin line of white smoke was rising up.

'Oh no.'

Felix took a step back and looked around her. But there was no point trying to run. She knew from before that the smoke was too quick for her. Where had it come from? Inside the crystal?

Felix tensed as the smoke travelled up towards her face. She waited for it to envelop her and squeeze her like a snake suffocating its prey.

When it reached her face, though, it stopped and floated in the air.

'Go on, what are you waiting for?'

The smoke continued to hover, reminding Felix of how Wrigglesworth's smoke had floated in front of him. He had whispered something to it and it had then attacked her.

'Are … are you waiting for me to tell you what to do?'

It might have been her imagination, but the smoke seemed to glow in response.

Shaking slightly, she reached out to cup the smoke in her hands. It let her and she felt its warmth against her skin.

'Find Tristan Traiton. Tie him to the wheel of *The Relampagos* and force the ship to steer north.'

Felix didn't honestly think this would work, but with Thistlewick about to be destroyed and nothing else left to try, it was worth a shot.

She opened her hands up wide, like Wrigglesworth had done, and the smoke rose up into the air. In a flash it was away, soaring across the fields.

Felix's mouth fell open. 'It worked… It worked!'

She ran after the smoke, towards the eastern edge of Thistlewick.

43

Crash!

Luna focused hard on the crystal ball. The image still flickered, but as Traiton started to turn the ship around, it grew stronger.

Caspar! Caspar!

Luna saw his eyes deaden. He had heard her and was ready to be instructed.

Take the bomb into the cave, then set it to detonate!

Caspar gave the other children their orders and they headed in through the cave entrance.

'Arrrgggghhh!'

Luna looked up. It was Traiton. For a second it looked like he was swatting flies, but his body froze and Luna noticed the white smoke that wound around him.

'Get it off me! Get it off!'

'Wrigglesworth!' Luna called. 'Why have you set your smoke on Traiton again?'

The ghost floated next to her, open-mouthed. 'That … this isn't my smoke.' He turned slowly to Luna. 'You said that Storm smashed the girl's crystal ball.'

'Oh no.' Luna's eyes widened as she realised what he meant. She watched the smoke curling around Traiton's arms and attaching his hands to the ship's wheel.

'Do something, Wrigglesworth!' Traiton yelled.

'T-there's nothing I can do, sir. That smoke has come from the crystal ball the girl was using. It will only answer to her.'

'Arrrggghhh!' Traiton cried again as the smoke forced his hands to turn the ship back round to sail north.

'Wrigglesworth, come and help me,' said Luna, her heart beating fast.

She ran over to the wheel and tried pulling it the opposite way to the smoke. Wrigglesworth joined her and even his dog grabbed the wheel with its mouth. But the three of them were no match for the smoke.

It swung the wheel furiously around, sending Luna flying backwards onto the deck. The ship was now facing north and cutting through the angry waves.

Luna watched Traiton trying desperately to rip himself away from the smoke, but this only made it tighten its grip.

'No!' Traiton roared. 'No! No! NO!'

'What is it?' asked Luna.

'Rocks ahead!' called Wrigglesworth.

Luna stood up and saw several large, pointed rocks lurking directly in the path of *The Relampagos*, like giant shark fins.

She looked from Wrigglesworth to Traiton.

He stared up to the sky. 'Curse you, Felix Dashwood!'

CRASH!

Traitor Traiton

Felix reached the edge of the cliff just in time to see *The Relampagos* hitting one of the many sharp rocks that surrounded Shark Fin Cove.

She swept her rain-drenched hair from her eyes and watched as the rock pierced a giant hole in the side of the ship. *The Relampagos* fell to its right, its masts splintering instantly on the rocks. Waves lapped up around the ship and started to eat away at it.

A beam of light shot out of the ship and through the rain then, and Felix saw at the centre of it the glow of two creatures. It was Wrigglesworth and his dog, fleeing before the ship went down. There was no sign of Traiton or Luna Claw, though.

Did this mean that their control over Thistlewick had ended?

Felix took out her walkie-talkie. 'Drift?' Drift?'

There was no reply.

Felix took one final look at the sinking ship, swung around and charged back across Thistlewick.

***

Felix saw fires burning through the houses along several lanes as she and Mrs Didsbury's dogs arrived back in South Thistlewick.

They ran the rest of the way to the market. Felix shielded her eyes at the brightness of the sight that met her as she turned into the market square. The thatched roofs of all the buildings were ablaze, shooting yellow and white sparks all over the place, which in turn hit the trees and set fire to them too.

Felix saw Drift sitting outside the church, against a gravestone, tied to it with rope.

'Drift!' She went over and started to untie him.

'What's happening, Felix? The ship? The bomb?'

'I think I've managed to stop them,' she replied.

Drift frowned. 'How?'

'I'll explain in a bit.'

She looked up at the church entrance. The big oak door opened and several islanders stepped out, blinking and shaking their heads.

Felix breathed a huge sigh of relief. 'We've done it, Drift. Luna Claw definitely isn't controlling them any more.'

'What on earth has been happening? It feels like I have been asleep,' said Mrs Spindle.

'Fire!' yelled Mr Finch.

Farmer Potts rushed out of the church. 'How did this happen?'

Felix ran over. 'It was while you were all in the church. The market's on fire and so are lots of the houses to the east.'

The farmer nodded. 'Children, stay away from the fire. Everyone else, I'm going to need all the help I can get. Come with me!'

He ran off, followed by a dozen islanders.

'Hey,' a voice came from behind Felix.

She turned to see Caspar standing there.

'Caspar,' she said, slightly warily. 'What's happened to the bomb?'

'I-I,' he stuttered. 'I don't know what's been going on for the past few days, but I just found myself standing in a cave staring down at this small metal ball. Rocco told me it was a bomb and asked if he should detonate it.'

'And did he?'

'No! I told him not to. We've just left it there.' He looked around them in horror. 'Why is the market on fire?'

Felix hugged him tightly, ignoring his confused look – he was his old self again.

'It's a long story, mate,' said Drift.

The three of them watched as Farmer Potts gathered

up his hose and started to shoot water at the fire. Other islanders set up a relay, and Felix, Caspar and Drift helped them carry buckets of water to the market.

Once Felix was sure Farmer Potts had everything under control, she turned to Drift and Caspar. 'Come with me. There's something you need to see. I'll explain it all on the way, Caspar.'

***

Felix, Caspar and Drift leant over Traiton. He lay in Shark Fin Cove, covered in seaweed and sand, his eyes closed.

'He is still alive, isn't he?' asked Caspar.

'Yeah, he's breathing.' Drift pointed.

Felix looked around. The wreck of the ship was still bashing in between the rocks and planks of wood had washed up onto the beach. Just along from Traiton was a pile of dark blue cloth. Mrs Didsbury's dogs were sniffing around it.

Felix went over and grabbed hold of the cloth. She realised it was a cloak – just like Luna Claw's. She pulled it up, and out rolled a shining, see-through ball.

'Look!' said Felix. 'That must be Luna Claw's crystal ball. There's no sign of Luna, though. I wonder—'

She was interrupted by coughing and spluttering. Traiton was coming round. She walked back over to the others as the man blinked and glared up at them.

He frowned his devil-horn eyebrows at Felix. 'You!'

'Hello, again, Traitor Traiton.'

Drift waved at him and even Caspar grinned down.

'So there was nothing we could do to stop you destroying Thistlewick, was there? Do you still think you can get your revenge on me?' asked Felix.

Traiton glanced around. 'Where am I?'

'Shark Fin Cove,' said Drift.

'The same place your great-great-great-great-grandfather wrecked his ship in 1880,' Caspar pointed out.

'Face it, Traitor Traiton, we've beaten you again!' Felix said triumphantly.

Traiton's eyes became black pins. He gritted his teeth and started to get up, a low growl coming from his mouth. Felix and Drift took a step back uncertainly; Caspar took three.

Traiton's growl was matched by Mrs Didsbury's dogs. Felix glanced over – all four of them were focused on the crystal ball. She could just see inside it an image of Traiton's head. The dogs began yapping at the ball, a high-pitched sound that bounced around the cove.

Traiton, on his knees, looked at them. 'What the…?'

Then his face went blank. A few seconds later he opened his mouth and a strange sound came out.

'Ah rooff! Rooff! ROOFF!'

Ignoring the children, he moved onto all fours. Felix frowned, unsure what was happening.

Mrs Didsbury's dogs looked at Traiton and tilted their heads curiously. Then they wagged their tails and trotted over to him.

'They think he's a dog like them,' said Drift.

'I think he thinks he's a dog too,' said Caspar, as Traiton hung his tongue out and began to pant.

'The crystal ball must understand dog talk,' said Felix. 'When Mrs Didsbury's dogs barked into it, they must have been telling Traiton to act like them.'

Felix, Caspar and Drift watched with baffled amusement as Traiton and the dogs chased each other around the beach. It was when Traiton started spinning around, chasing what he thought was his own tail, that Felix couldn't hold it in any longer.

She burst out laughing, followed quickly by Drift and Caspar, their happy, relieved sounds echoing around Shark Fin Cove.

The Wedding

'I now, finally, pronounce you man and wife!' said the vicar the next day.

A cheer rang around the church and Felix clapped along with everyone else.

As Mayor and Mrs Merryweather walked back down the isle to organ music, beaming at everyone in sight, Felix chuckled about Traiton again.

When the police had arrived in their boat yesterday, Traiton was still acting like a dog, even through Mrs Didsbury's dogs had stopped barking at the crystal ball. None of the police officers had had the slightest idea about how to snap Traiton out of it and Felix decided not to tell them about the crystal ball. In the end, the police didn't have to handcuff him or chain him up. They got him onto their boat by throwing a bone for him to chase after.

Felix had told the police about the bomb, although she didn't mention anything about how Mr Tweedale, Caspar or the other children were involved. She just said she had heard Traiton talking about it. Soon, a special bomb squad had arrived at the island to remove it.

No one really remembered what had happened when they were being controlled by Luna Claw, and they had assumed the fires around Thistlewick had been caused by lightning during the storm. Some of the buildings had been badly damaged and would need repairing, but Farmer Potts's skills had prevented them from being completely destroyed.

After the wedding, everyone milled around outside the church. Felix was with her mum when Mr Tweedale walked up to them.

'Well, Mrs Dashwood,' he said. 'I believe I excluded your daughter, but I honestly cannot think what for.' He turned to Felix and smiled. 'You proved yourself a hero yesterday, finding Tristan Traiton again, so you are very welcome to come back to school.'

'Thanks,' she said, returning his smile.

Mrs Didsbury hobbled past them then and Felix thought about the crystal ball she had taken from Shark Fin Cove. It wasn't Mrs Didsbury's, of course – that would forever stay smashed into a thousand pieces scattered around North Thistlewick. This was Luna Claw's crystal ball, but it looked identical to Mrs Didsbury's, so she would never know the difference.

Felix looked to Mum. 'Is it OK if I go home, Mum? There's something in my room that I need to return to someone.'

'Of course,' said Mum, and Felix left her chatting with Mr Tweedale.

***

'What is it?' asked Mrs Didsbury through the crack in her front door.

'I've got something for your dogs,' replied Felix.

'What?'

'Bones. They were really good on our walk yesterday, so I thought they deserved a treat.'

Mrs Didsbury narrowed her eyes. 'I do not want them getting fat. But seeing as you are here, you might as well come in. The dogs are in their basket.'

Felix followed the old lady in. When they walked into the living room, the dogs all looked up lazily.

'Dogs, I have bones for you.' Felix took four long, white objects out of her pocket.

Suddenly the dogs sprang into life. They clambered over each other to get out of the basket, jumping up and spinning round in excited circles.

'Well, I have never seen them so lively,' said Mrs Didsbury, shaking her head.

Felix gave each dog a bone and they were soon busy chewing them on the floor.

'Can I use your toilet?' Felix asked Mrs Didsbury.

'If you must. You know where it is.'

Felix left the room and walked up the stairs. But instead of turning left into the bathroom, she walked right into Mrs Didsbury's bedroom. Felix pulled open the door of the bedside cabinet and removed all the magazines. She unzipped her bag, took out Luna's crystal ball and carefully placed it in the cabinet.

'Aha!'

Felix jumped and turned around. Mrs Didsbury stood in the doorway, arms folded.

'I knew it! I knew you were up to no good.'

'Sorry, Mrs Didsbury, I … I was just borrowing it.'

'Like you tried to *borrow* my boat too?'

'There was a very important reason I took it.'

'Ha! A likely story!' Mrs Didsbury shook her head. 'Once a thief, always a thief. You will leave my house this instant. And if I hear that you have mentioned one word about my past to anyone, you really will be sorry. Understand?' Her voice had become shrill and high by the end of this speech.

'Yes, Mrs Didsbury.'

'Then get out, thief!'

As Felix left number 7, Featherbed Lane, she smiled. Now she had been called a hero and a thief within the space of a few minutes.

Even when you've saved Thistlewick from destruction, she told herself, *some things never change!*

Epilogue

'Goodnight, dogs,' said Seraphina Didsbury later that evening as she covered the four mounds of fluff with a blanket.

She climbed the stairs, shut the bedroom curtains and was soon in bed herself. After a few minutes a faint snore came out of her mouth. She was fast asleep.

From the edges of the bedside cabinet door, a glow appeared. It grew brighter and brighter, until the room was filled with light.

But still Seraphina slept.

Inside the cabinet, blue sparks shot out from the crystal ball. The silvery smoke swirled around and around inside it, gradually revealing a face. A face full of loathing and anger, with blood-red eyes and arched eyebrows.

There, inside Seraphina Didsbury's bedside cabinet, Luna waited.

Soon she would have her revenge!

Read Felix's other adventures in book 1...

1880: In an intense battle the fearsome pirate, Captain Traiton, captures the great ship, *Tormenta*. But waiting onboard is an unexpected surprise, which will lead to Traiton's downfall.

Today: Stuck in detention, Felix is bored, until she finds a note written by her evil head teacher, Mr Foxsworth, which mentions treasure on Thistlewick Island.

Can Felix, Caspar and Drift, find the treasure before Mr Foxsworth gets it? What is his connection to Captain Traiton? And what will happen when the past and the present collide?

Visit the website to find out more!

... and in book 2!

50 years ago:
Amelie is trapped in her bedroom in Murkhill Mansion, with only her diary and her rag toys to keep her company.

Today:
When exploring the abandoned Murkhill Mansion, Felix, Caspar and Drift find Amelie's diary. Strange things start to happen – the rooms mix themselves up in an impossible maze and the mansion turns into a nightmare world that the children cannot escape from. Then Drift goes missing.

Everything that is happening seems to be connected to Amelie and her diary. But what is turning her nightmares into reality? Can Felix and Caspar find Drift? And what will happen when Amelie's rag toys mutate into something far creepier and more dangerous?

www.luketemple.co.uk

Luke Temple's 'Ghost Island' series:

When the world-famous ghost hunter, Spooky Steve, investigates Becky's home above the post office, the ghost of Walter Anion appears and curses the place. Can Becky figure out how to stop this curse, before everything she knows and loves is destroyed forever?

Becky and Finn get trapped inside the abandoned Thicket House by a monsterous ghost, known as 'the spectre'. As the spectre's evil plans become clear, they have to battle their fears and fight for their lives. Can they escape from Thicket House before it's too late?

www.luketemple.co.uk

An exclusive interview with Luke Temple

Q: *Who is your favourite character in the 'Felix Dashwood' series?*

A: Felix! I would love to be as adventurous as her. My favourite baddie is Tristan Traiton, which is why I decided he had to return in book 3.

Q: *Which is your favourite chapter in the whole of the 'Felix Dashwood' series?*

A: I really like the chapter with the flying tortoises in *Mutating Mansion*. But my favourite has to be chapter 44 in *Traitor's Revenge*, when Tristan Traiton is hypnotised into thinking he's a dog...

At the end of *Traitor's Treasure* he gets sent back to prison, so the same thing couldn't happen again in *Traitor's Revenge*. I had to think of a new way of giving him his comeuppance. I laughed a lot when I thought of the 'dog' idea and I have been looking forward to writing it for a long time!

Q: *What is your favourite word?*

A: 'Syzygy' – because no one ever guesses how to spell it. Also, 'comeuppance' is quite fun.

Q: *If you could visit anywhere on Thistlewick Island, where would you go?*

A: I'd happily spend a few hours down in the harbour hut, listening to Albert the fisherman tell stories. There's also a mysterious ship on top of a cliff in North Thistlewick. It's been there ever since I created the island and I still don't know why! I'd love to explore that ship, even though there are rumours that it might be cursed...

Q: *How long does it take you to write a book?*

A: Some books take about a year and a half to write. Others, like *Mutating Mansion*, only take a couple of months! I don't spend that much time actually writing, though. Most of the time I'm just letting ideas build up in my head.

Q: *What is the worst thing you have ever written?*

A: I once tried to write a book about Albert the fisherman turning into a talking fish. I got about half way through, then realised that it was a very silly idea.

An exclusive interview with illustrator Jessica Chiba

Q: *How did you decide what Felix, Caspar and Drift would look like?*

A: I had a clear image in my head of what they would look like when I first read the story. I wanted Felix to look like a daring tomboy, but with dramatic long hair she puts in a ponytail to keep out of the way. I wanted Caspar to look less sporty, like his mother had dressed him. Drift had to be a bit more slouchy and cool in his attitude, with scruffy hair.

Q: *Which is your favourite illustration in the whole series?*

A: A difficult question! I think I like the dragon in *Mutating Mansion* best, although I like the way the mansion came out too.

Q: *How long does it take you to draw each full-page illustration? What about the book covers?*

A: An illustration can take 8 to 24 hours. It depends on whether I have to draw difficult things like rundown houses and pirate ships. There's less drawing to do on the covers, so they can take a little less time, but including the colouring and the titles they take about 8 hours.

Q: *What is your favourite thing to draw?*

A: I like drawing people. I enjoy drawing their expressions and eyes.

Q: *What is your least favourite thing to draw?*

A: Another difficult question! I prefer drawing living things, so I suppose I don't enjoy drawing houses and ships as much as people. After all the ships I had to draw for the 'Felix Dashwood' series, I've had enough of them for a while, I think. Too many ropes!

Q: *What else do you do, other than illustrate Luke Temple's books?*

A: I do many things! I draw comics and pictures, I read lots of books, I play the violin and I study and teach at a university.

These are Jessica's very first sketches of Felix, Caspar and Drift!

To find out more about how Luke and Jessica wrote and illustrated the 'Felix Dashwood' series, including fun videos and hidden secrets, visit the website:

www.luketemple.co.uk